A Hustler's SON II

Live Or Die In New York...

THE SEQUEL TO A HUSTLER'S SON

BY T. STYLES

Library of Congress Control Number: 2008902101
ISBN: 0-9794931-5-3
ISBN 13: 978-0-9794931-5-7
Cover Design: Davida Baldwin www.oddballdsgn.com
Editor: Advance Editorial Services
Graphics: Davida Baldwin
Typesetting: Davida Baldwin
First Edition
Printed in the United States of America

DEDICATIONS

This novel is dedicated to Charisse Washington.
Only you really knew what I went through mentally, and physi-
cally to write this book. I am eternally grateful for you.

ACKNOWLEDGMENT

Wow...I did it!

It's finally here!

This novel took a lot out of me. Why? I can't really say. Part of me believes it has everything to do with not wanting to let my fans down. And the other part of me feels it's because this story launched my career. I wanted to give my fans who appreciated the original storyline an even better novel. With that said, I'd like to thank my loyal fans, who are my reason for writing. You guys are the best. You mean everything to me.

In the past I've thanked people who didn't necessarily play a significant role in the production of my novels. With this novel, I'd like to thank those who contributed directly to me completing this story.

Charisse, thank you for always reading my creations and giving me feedback whether good or bad. You're the one who motivated me to keep Kelsi alive. And you are the one I didn't want to let down. I love you! From the bottom of my heart. I hope you know and can feel that.

Kajel, my son, my only child, thank you for running Cartel Café & Books, our newest investment, while I focused on this novel. You make me proud to see you in action. You were amazing at the Harlem Book Fair! Always remember to keep God first, and believe in yourself. You're the best.

Jason Poole. Thanks for taking me away from the worries of business to enjoy life and have fun.

Eyone Williams, my author, you continuously stay upbeat despite being confined. You are a literary genius! A phenomenal writer, and an even better spirit.

Anthony Fields, I call you the author who can write a hot book on command! What can I say…your skills are not to be phucked with! I feel honored to publish your newest creation.

To K.D. Harris, my author, you're the best sweetheart! I love your energy! And you are sick with the pen! Keep strokin'! And thanks for holding the Cartel down!

To V.J. Gotastory, my author, who has singlehandedly supported every Cartel event with a warm smile, and love! You're the best! I don't think the world can wait for your novel, Year Of The Crackmom! Get 'em girl!

To CeeCee and Angel! You guys are the heart of the Cartel. Doing what you can for the business because you love us, and you're family. Thanks for being a part of my life.

To DJ Phreakshow, the Cartel DJ, thanks for drawing in the crowds and putting the swag in my hips with your music at our store.

To Monica, my closest and oldest friend, thanks for always supporting me. You are a breath of fresh air. I smile whenever I see your face.

To Giovanna, thanks for giving us the pic to make the Pitbulls In A Skirt cover complete. And most of all, thanks for being my friend, I adore you.

To Davida, the Cartel's graphic designer, what can I say, you're the best love! Whatever you do comes to life! Thank you! And I know, without a doubt, that your mother is proud and honored to have a daughter like you. She's in a better place. My soul is sure of it.

If I forgot you, hold it to my mind and not my heart.

T. Styles
President & CEO, The Cartel Publications
www.thecartelpublications.com
www.myspace.com/toystyles.com

What's Good Fam,

First off, I gotta say thank you all so much for your continued support. Everything we do at "The Cartel" we do for each and every one of you. 2008 was our premier year, and we came out swingin'…Oh but 2009, that shit goin' be even more fire!! We comin' wit' the sequels ya'll been blowin' my phone up for, some new shit ya'll goin' love *annnnd* we comin' with part 2 of a classic that you ain't goin' even believe 'til you read it. Trust me, The Cartel is here to stay and we ain't goin' no where!

Now…. A Hustler's Son 2, I personally could not wait for this joint! I love every single book T. has penned, straight up, but I'd be bullshittin' if I ain't tell you that A Hustler's Son was my favorite. That joint was it for me for several reasons, but what I loved the most was Kelsi was a thorough lil nigga!! In this joint, my man is pissed! He gotta lot of hurt and pain in his heart, so he bringin' it straight to the bammas that caused it, or so he thinks. So cut the phone off, put the babies to bed and get ya read in. You'll be happy that you did.

I can't end this letter without shoutin' out the author we honor. It is my pleasure to pay homage to none other than:

"Quentin Carter"

Not only is Quentin Carter T. Styles' favorite author, and she will tell you that straight up if you ask, this dude is en fuego (fire)!!! I love how Quentin tells a story. If you don't know, Quentin is the author of, "Hoodwinked", "In Cahootz", "Amongst Thieves", "Stained Cotton" and "The Fink" which is a short story in the anthology, "Street Love" which T. Styles also contributed to. The Cartel loves Quentin Carter and once you crack open one his books, you'll see why.

Thanks for lettin' me rap to you. Go on and get ya read on. I'ma get at you next time. Don't forget, if you in the DMV (DC, Maryland, Virginia) area, come check out, Cartel Café' & Books located at 5011 B Indian Head Highway Oxon Hill, MD. If you not in that area, don't worry we comin' to a city near you.

Be easy!!

Charisse "C Wash" Washington
VP, The Cartel Publications
www.thecartelpublications.com

A HUSTLER'S SON RECAP

CHAPTER ONE

Janet Stayley is in bed masturbating when her on and off boyfriend Delonte knocks on the door. It's 3 in the morning and she's startled thinking somebody has died or something tragic has happened. Prior to that, she kicked Delonte out of her apartment because she caught him in the car kissing his cousin Kenosha. When Janet surrenders and opens the door, Kelsi is angry and expresses it in the way he disrespects him.

CHAPTER TWO

Kelsi and his friend Bricks walks to school talking about how he disrespected Delonte the night before, by implying that he'd kick his ass if he steps out of line. The boys find humor in the matter and go on to talk about Kelsi's girlfriend Lakeisha. Once at school, Kelsi gets into it with Keisha's ex-boyfriend Charles who never got over her and hates seeing the two of them together. Kelsi clowns him in front of everybody and she leaves on his arm. Later while walking home from school he holds Kelsi at gunpoint strikes him and kidnaps Keisha. Kelsi goes home and solicits Bricks and his brother Melvin's help. When they finally catch up with Charles at a mall parking lot, Keisha isn't with him. Angered, he pistol whips Charles as Bricks and Melvin watch. When he returns home, Janet's boyfriend Delonte is there and attempting to play the father roll when he sees the bruises on his face from fighting Charles. Kelsi jumps in his face and reminds him that he is not his son and he doesn't respect or fear him. Kelsi challenges him and Delonte backs down. Disgusted by his weakness, Kelsi hates him even more.

CHAPTER THREE

Janet comes home from work exhausted. Right before she enters her apartment, Charles approaches her and gives Janet a message for her son. Although the message appears harmless, Charles knows that once Kelsi finds out he approached his mother, he'd be furious. Once inside her home, she senses the tension between Delonte and Kelsi. When she tries to find out what went wrong, they argue again and she removes Kelsi from the situation by taking him into his room. In Kelsi's room she gets a sense of how much he cares for her by looking at the pictures of her over his room. It's clear that their bond is unbreakable.

CHAPTER FOUR

Kelsi goes to a party with Bricks at a local fire department. The entire time he's there, Charles is on his mind. He knows the altercation they had is far from over. And…he can't wait to get to Keisha, who's at his house waiting on him in his room. She's not fully alone. Delonte is there. And Kelsi forbade her to leave his room believing Delonte's attracted to her. When he and Bricks leave the party, to drop him off home, Bricks reminds him that he has his back no matter what. Once he's dropped off, Kelsi leaves the car and walks into the night, the moment he does, Charles approaches him.

CHAPTER FIVE

Kelsi kills Charles in self defense and dumps his body in a trash bin outside of his apartment. With blood covering his body, he enters the apartment and is enraged when he sees Keisha on the couch talking to Delonte. He sends her to his room and threatens Delonte again. As usual, Delonte backs off and Kelsi and Keisha enter his room. He chastises her for not listening but lightens his mood when he senses her worry about him. Although Keisha wants to know what happened to Kelsi since he's covered in blood, he doesn't confide in her about the murder. Angry at Kelsi's continuous disrespect, Delonte calls Janet at work saying Kelsi came home covered in blood. And when she asks to speak to Kelsi, he refuses to come to the phone. He wants Delonte to know he's not moved by him calling his mother. Instead, he lies in the bed with Keisha and has sex with her.

CHAPTER SIX

Janet comes home in a cab frustrated that Kelsi didn't come to the phone after she requested to speak to him. She can't understand why he and Delonte can't get along. She puts Keisha out of Kelsi's room and tells her to go into hers and wait for him. Then she gives Kelsi a piece of her mind with a bat in hand. She tells Kelsi how she wasn't as soft as he thought she was. Janet tells him that she was raped by her father and her brothers before fleeing. Later she got involved with a girl gang called the Monopoly Honeys. She went in to detail about how she met his father, Lorenzo, and how she slept with him with her best friend Shelly at the same time because Lorenzo wanted to see how down she really was for him. And, that Kelsi and Lorenzo Jr., Shelly's son, were conceived at the same time. Janet told Kelsi how Lorenzo beat Shelly so badly while pregnant, her son, Lorenzo came out retarded. Later Lorenzo chose Shelly and because of this, she and Shelly grew apart. Just when Kelsi thought he couldn't hear anymore, Janet explained how she moved to New York and met up with a man who tried to kill her. His name was never given. In the end Janet told Kelsi if he ever disrespected her again, she'd kill him. Kelsi visibly shaken, dropped his own bomb by telling her he killed someone earlier that night. Devastated, Janet told Kelsi no matter what, she was there for him. Even if it meant helping him cover up the murder. Their bond in crime is formed.

CHAPTER SEVEN

Learning her only son was a murderer weighed heavily on Janet. When she wakes up from a deep sleep she hears Delonte talking to someone on the phone. He made comments about Janet pacifying Kelsi too much. He went on to say he was going to find out something and Janet had a feeling it had to do with the murder of Charles. This enrages her and she makes a promise to do whatever she has to protect him. Even if it means killing Delonte.

CHAPTER EIGHT

Kelsi has a lot on his mind after hearing everything his mother said to him the night before. Her being raped and almost killed was a lot for him to take all at once. While walking Keisha to the bus stop, she yaps over and over again about nothing. Kelsi chokes Keisha up because her talking prevents him from thinking straight. With killing Charles and hearing about his mother's past, he wasn't in his right state of mind. When he realizes he could possibly kill her, he releases the hold he has on her throat. He warns her about being with him, but she stays true accepting his abuse. Still, he doesn't trust himself around her.

CHAPTER NINE

When Janet comes home for work, she tells Kelsi that they must kill Delonte. She's worried if they don't, he'll tell someone about Kelsi murdering Charles. Although she doesn't believe Delonte's knows the facts, she doesn't want to take the chance. Kelsi thinks his mother is crazy and wants to make sure he's not a suspect in the first murder before committing another one. In the end, he refuses.

CHAPTER TEN

Kelsi is in class thinking about his mother's request to kill Delonte. When he learns over the school intercom that Charles body has been found he becomes nervous. The teacher refuses to let him leave the room after he requests. When Kelsi disrespects the teacher, he leaves anyway and hooks up with Keisha. They leave school early and walk home together. Before stopping home, he calls Skully, his drug connect, from a convenience store payphone. Kelsi tells him that someone was murdered in the area Kelsi sells drugs in and that things may be too hot to pump. His connect demands he stays low key until things cool off. Kelsi obeys gets off the phone and goes home. With Keisha on his arm, they run into Kenosha, Delonte's sexy cousin. He sends Keisha upstairs to talk to Kenosha alone. Keisha is angry but obeys not wanting to upset Kelsi again after getting on his nerves the day before. Kenosha offers Kelsi up sexually and he flirts but declines. Once he goes inside his apartment, Keisha hands him a card and runs into the house. She's upset. Kelsi's afraid after looking at the card knowing Keisha, in her naïve state, said too much.

CHAPTER ELEVEN

Janet walks in and overhears Kelsi and Keisha's conversation. Keisha tells Kelsi that she told the police that he had a fight with Charles before he was murdered. Janet enters Kelsi's room and sends Keisha home so that she can talk to Kelsi alone. She's angered that Keisha is so stupid and that her son's freedom may now be at risk.

CHAPTER TWELVE

Kelsi walks to school with Bricks the next day and tells him about Keisha's slip up with the police. Bricks attempts to comfort him by saying that as long as she didn't say anything specific, he should be okay. Kelsi is still uneasy. Once at school, Kelsi notices Delonte's truck. Delonte tells him to get inside and blackmails him. Delonte goes into detail about how Skully cut him off and now he's no longer able to service his customers in the Woods, the same complex Kelsi hustles and lives in. Now, he wants Kelsi to sell drugs for him in Skully's neighborhood. If Kelsi doesn't, he threatens to tell the police the little he knows about him coming home the day Charles was murdered, covered in blood. Kelsi refuses believing he doesn't have enough proof to cause him any harm. Until Charles reveals he has the blood stained shirt he wore the night of the murder. Angered and defeated, Kelsi realizes his mother was right all along. And he agrees murdering Delonte will be best for them all.

CHAPTER THIRTEEN

Janet was ending a private conversation when Delonte walked in on her. Although he didn't hear the entire conversation, he had a feeling it was about him. When he asked Janet what the call was about, she brushed him off. Angry, he had sex with her at gunpoint. What scared him was that Janet enjoyed it. In her mind she was giving herself as a dead man's final wish. Kelsi was at the door and watched their entire sexual encounter.

CHAPTER FOURTEEN

Janet and Delonte carry out their plans to kill Delonte. Afterwards, they dump his body in a park. With the night as their only witness, they pledge their lives together. And above all, they vow to keep each other's secret.

CHAPTER FIFTEEN

Kelsi goes to Delonte's house with Kenosha and has to endure seeing the pain in Delonte's mother's face. Delonte's mother was certain something terrible happened to him since he hadn't been home. Kenosha appears to be visibly shaken by Delonte's death too. Eventually Mrs. Knight leaves Kelsi and Kenosha, who is staying with them from time to time, alone. Kelsi is there to get any money or drugs he may have had stashed since he knew Delonte was never coming back. In the process of roaming in his room, he finds nothing. He knew someone beat him to it. But who? Kenosha walked up on him during his search. He played it off like he went upstairs in the hopes she'd follow him, so they could have sex. And they did, raw.

CHAPTER SIXTEEN

Janet is upset that Kelsi is with Kenosha. She doesn't trust her. Part of it has to do with her sleeping with Delonte, a man she loved at one time. And the other part of it had to do with Delonte being her cousin. If she was that careless to get who she wanted, who knew what she might do to conceive her young son. Janet didn't want her anywhere near her son. While on the phone with Kelsi, Keisha clicks in and Janet develops another plan. To rid her son of Keisha, who she believes is weak; she formed an instant full proof plan. Janet secretly didn't want any woman around Kelsi but herself. So Janet convinces Keisha to give Kelsi a hard time by seeming uninterested. She says if she does, Kelsi would want her even more. Keisha is persuaded in following her advice and Janet tells her Kelsi's best friend Bricks would be the perfect candidate to make Kelsi jealous. After she hangs up with Keisha, she examines her bullet ridden body and remembers how Jarvis, her ex-boyfriend in New York, attempted to kill her. But she manages to escape, and Skully is the one who helped her.

CHAPTER SEVENTEEN

Janet decides she wants to get back in the drug game so that she and Kelsi can escape all together. So she calls Skully and expresses her interests. He warns her against dealing business with him. He made it clear that he is not the same person she knew when it came to his money. He could be ruthless, but she insists. He doesn't want to mix business with their friendship. Because since he saved her life, he looked out for her. And…even made sure her only son Kelsi worked for him to prevent him from getting mixed up with the wrong dealers. Skully eventually agrees to go in business with her and their call is over. Later detective Nick Fearson knocks on the door questioning Janet about the murder of Charles. When she's unhelpful, he vows to bring her and her son down.

CHAPTER EIGHTEEN

Kelsi feels on top of the world having recently slept with Kenosha. He goes to school and tries to talk to his girlfriend Keisha. She's talking to Bricks and ignores him in the hallway. He's embarrassed and tries to conceal his anger from his friend. He asks him what were they talking about and Bricks tells him that she was speaking of some talk show. His response makes him suspect that he wants to get with Keisha. Kelsi flips the script on Keisha in class by talking to some other girls and this breaks her down. She tries to make up with him unable to play the game, but Kelsi gives her a taste of her own medicine by ignoring her. At home, Kelsi learns from his mother that Skully and his mother knew each other. He also discovers he saved his mother's life. Janet also shares with him that she knew he sold drugs. Kelsi feels betrayed. He also learns more about what happened to his mother in New York before she was shot, and associates the name Jarvis and Kyopes with her troubles. Most important, Janet tells Kelsi her next idea to murder his father,

Lorenzo for the insurance money. Kelsi is left breathless realizing the cold blooded person his mother truly is.

CHAPTER NINETEEN

Janet calls Shelly and asks her to care for Kelsi if something happens to her. Shelly is confused at first by her request because Janet doesn't like her and she knows it. She eventually agrees. Later Kelsi wants answers from his mother. He wants to know why she allowed him to sell drugs. He feels used. Like she doesn't care. Janet tells him that she knew he would sell no matter what she wanted and the least she could do was make sure he got them from the right person. Later Kelsi tells his mother what's really on his mind. Kelsi believes Keisha is sleeping with his best friend Bricks. Janet confirms his beliefs by saying she saw them together in public. Kelsi is hurt and vows to cut them both off for good. Wanting to take his murder out on someone, he agrees to help his mother murder his father.

CHAPTER TWENTY

Kelsi goes to school with hate in his heart for Bricks and Keisha after hearing what his mother said. He was clueless that his mother set Keisha up. Keisha still unable to take Kelsi's rejection agrees to give Kelsi oral sex in the boy's bathroom when he demands. And when she does, he treats her like a whore. Feeling like she lost him for good, she's seconds from telling Kelsi that it was his mother who told her to pretend to be with Bricks, but he chokes her over the pure mentioning of his mother's name. He leaves her at school, and jumps in the car with Kenosha. Keisha sees this and breaks down in tears.

CHAPTER TWENTY-ONE

With the plan to kill Lorenzo in place, Kelsi waits for his mother at a DC park. She was supposed to lure Lorenzo there and together they would kill him for the insurance money. But...his mother never shows. Realizing it was unlike her, he grows worried. It didn't help matters that Bricks kept calling while he waited on his mother's call. Anxious, he's furious when he see's Keisha pull up. She'd been following him the entire time. He tells her to leave several times but she demands he talks to her. Kelsi knew she couldn't be around when his mother came with Lorenzo so again he warned her to leave. When she didn't he killed her and through her lifeless body in the ocean. With adrenaline coursing through his veins, and fearing the worse, he says aloud, "Mama, if you can hear me, I love you. I need you to know that I love you."

CHAPTER TWENTY-TWO

Skully and Kenosha kidnapped Janet and had her bound on a basement floor. She'd been beaten badly. She never knew Skully held resentment for her. Turns out she treated him badly when she was with Jarvis and he never got over it. He only pretended to like her to eventually get back at her. Also, it's revealed that Jarvis stole from Skully on numerous occasions. That's the only reason he helped Janet to get away. He wanted unsaid revenge against Jarvis. And because of it, Skully wanted to have him killed and would use Kelsi. Janet also learns that they plan to have Kelsi do it by telling him after she was killed, that Jarvis killed her. Knowing he would believe Skully since she told Kelsi how he saved her life, she felt all was lost. Skully pumped three bullets in Janet's body.

CHAPTER TWENTY-THREE

Kenosha tells how she was not as dumb as everybody thought she was, and that she didn't care she was fucking her cousin Delonte. She says how she'll do whatever Skully wants her to for

that old mighty dollar, including ensuring that Kelsi goes through
with his plan to kill Jarvis.

CHAPTER TWENTY-FOUR

Skully reveals that he'll do what he can, to make sure Kelsi kills
Jarvis. Including wrapping his young mind up with lies, knowing
full well that he'll see him as a friend since the those were a few
of the last words he'd heard from his mother.

FINAL CHAPTER

On Christmas day, while grieving over the lost of his mother, he's
delivered a bloody heart. When he opens the package, he reads
the words, 'nobody has heart when they're dead'. Thinking
Jarvis is taunting him, he gets his whereabouts from Skully,
board a New York bus, and leaves to find him.

Now......we introduce to you
A Hustler's Son 2
Live or Die In New York

PROLOGUE

"Roc Boys" by Jay Z, blared from the speakers in the private party that Jarvis and Kyope threw for themselves. The room was dark with the exception of a few strobe lights while smoke hovered over the room like clouds in the sky before a thunderstorm.

Jarvis and Kyope sat next to each other in separate chairs with small round tables in front of them. Every once and awhile they'd nod at one another in approval for all they'd accomplished. Money dressed the tables like promotional flyers with no purpose. Everything was paid for and it was all because of them. It took Jarvis and Kyope forever to get to this point, but they could finally say that they were self-made billionaires.

While Kyope pulled on the best weed money could buy, Jarvis eyed Steel, his girlfriend of over three years as she sashayed across the dance floor. She was nicknamed Steel because her body looked as if it was built with the precision of a military assault weapon.

Every man in attendance looked at her small waist and thick ass while she danced and swayed her arms in the air. She was putting on quite a show for Jarvis. And her sex-appeal stood out like a naked female in a male prison. Her light skin wasn't as clear and flawless as it had been years back, but she was still a dime. Her golden locks fell over the tight-fitting white mini dress she wore by Loeffler Randall, and her black Christian Louboutin heels showcased her toned calves.

As good as life was, Jarvis had two problems. One…someone was stickin' up his shops for the past few months. And two…he'd recently learned that his girl was getting high on his supply. And had he been the only person aware, he'd probably cover for her somehow since one of Jarvis' flaws has always been a female. But she was caught red-handed by one of his trusted soldiers, and the situation had to be addressed.

"You aigh't, man?" Prangsta asked sitting in the available seat next to him. His long black dreads with bleach tips were pulled tightly into a long ponytail and stunk badly. His oversized pink lips were dry and cracked as usual.

Jarvis took a sip of the Remy VSOP in his glass, and pulled on his weed before taking another look at Steel. "You sure 'bout what you saw right?" Steel smiled at him and he winked back.

"That's my word, Jarvis. I met shawty at the warehouse like you asked me but I got there early. This bitch I went to see earlier wasn't fuckin' so I put her ass out on the Brooklyn Bridge and had time to burn." He laughed but Jarvis didn't. Clearing his throat he continued, "Anyway…she didn't see me walk up on her. She was diggin' in one of the keys from inside the book bag with a switch blade. She still had blow on her face when I knocked on the window."

What Prangsta didn't tell Jarvis was that she begged him not to tell and sucked his dick on the spot in the back seat of her red Mercedes so he wouldn't. Prangsta knew he'd never get a female of her caliber otherwise, so he took full advantage, but told Jarvis anyway excluding how he could now speak on the skills of her head game. Plus he knew once Jarvis found out she was getting high, anything she said would be worthless, even if it was the truth.

"How you gonna handle it?" Prangsta questioned.

Jarvis gave him a look that shook Prangsta so bad, he got up and left. He didn't feel the need to respond or answer his question. He was the boss, not the other way around.

After Prangsta removed himself from his table, he raised his glass to Kyope and took another sip. Although they were friends, Jarvis didn't tell him about his personal life because he was quite aware of how Kyope despised how he wifed women so quickly.

Focusing back on Steel, he noticed she'd just returned from the restroom. Instead of having the same swagger she had earlier, she appeared disoriented. Her steps mirrored that of a child who was trying to walk for the first time. One leg stagnated first and the other slowly followed. It was clear she had gotten high in the bathroom moments earlier.

Everyone stopped what they were doing and looked at her. Her eyes met Jarvis's before blood escaped from her nose and down her white expensive dress. A tear fell from her eyes shortly before she dropped to the floor.

While everyone rushed to her aide, Jarvis remained seated. He knew exactly what happened and felt no need to move. He'd placed battery acid in a key of his pure white before the party. He left it in clear view. And if it was true what Prangsta said, he knew she'd steal from him. And for her betrayal, the price was death. There was no way he could have a junky bitch on his arm, not even one he loved.

I ain't gonna tell you my whole life story, plus I ain't got time for that shit no way. Let's just say a few months ago, I was a different person. And if I make it outta New York alive, I doubt I'll ever be the same.
-Kelsi

MÓNDAY, 1:13 AM

****

Fuck Life! Right now...at this mothafuckin' moment,
I gotta be the most dangerous nigga alive. Believe dat!

-Keisl

Look at me.

Look at my fuckin' life.

I hate what I've become, but I can't remember who I use to be.

On my back, with my arms spread out on this dirty ass motel bed in Brooklyn, I think about how much more time I'd have to wait before I do what I came to do. The gray grungy carpet, dirty yellow curtains and broken T.V. shows the state of my world right now.

I feel grim.

I feel murderous.

I ain't showered in days and was still sportin' a white T,

wit' desert colored fatigues. I stared at the ceiling light so long, it started to blind me. Rubbin' my hand over my swollen knuckles, due to punchin' at the walls, I replayed over in my mind tomorrows' plan of action. *Finally* after followin' Kyope and Jarvis for months, I was preparin' to make my move. I coulda smoked both of them niggas a long time ago, but death is too easy. I wanted their lifestyles stripped away, and then their souls.

Even though housekeepin' was included wit' the cheap ass $30.00 a night spot I rented, I never let the maid inside my room. I trusted nothin' or no one. With my .45 next to me and a blunt in hand, I inhaled the smoke into my lungs. It took a second before I started feelin' its effects.

I felt light.

Calm.

And invincible.

For a moment I contemplated puttin' the gun to my head, and pullin' the trigger. Every day. And I do mean every fuckin' day my thoughts went from killin' myself to killin' them niggas. I usually had these feelin's while high. I'm walkin' around dead anyway. Why not end it all? I guess the only thing that kept me from pushin' off was revenge. I needed it...like I needed my dick.

I roam the streets of New York at night, half dead on my prowl. I'm so fucked up I could go on a murder spree and could care less about the consequences. Shit, I almost smoked two people a few hours ago when I went to grab somethin' to eat. One muthafucka asked me for directions, and the other accidentally bumped into me rushin' for a cab. If I don't push off on them niggas soon, I don't know what'll happen.

The water in the sink dripped loudly from the rusted bathroom faucet when I heard a light knock at the door. Sittin' up straight in the bed, I cocked my weapon and aimed in its direction. Seconds from smokin' towards the worn out wood, my eyes roamed to the last bullet I let off in the wall a few days back.

I'm nicked up and paranoid.

Instead of firin', I placed the fire from the blunt out on the floor and kicked it under the bed. Then I put on the smoke shades I always wore. I had to be a little smarter if I was gonna achieve my mission and poppin' guns in my room was likely to bring unnecessary attention.

"Who the fuck is it?!"

Silence.

"I said who's at the fuckin' door?!" No one answered and I tiptoed toward it fully prepared to blast.

Had Jarvis and Kyope found me before I'd gotten them?

"Kelsi, it's me. Kenosha." Her voice was soft and she sounded worried.

My muscles relaxed and my breathin' slowed down. Still…what the fuck was she doin' here? She wasn't supposed to come until tomorrow! Tuckin' the gun in the back of my fatigues, I pulled my shirt down to conceal it. Then I turned around to look at the room. There was no use tryin' to clean it.

It was a fucked up mess.

I was a fucked up mess.

If she wanted to pop up wit'out notice, she deserved to see exactly how I was livin'. She been blowin' up my cell phone ever since I gave her the new number. I changed it so that Shelly, the bitch my mother left to care for me after she was murdered, would stop callin, askin' me to come home. Wit' nothin' left to do but deal, I decided to check her right quick.

I opened the door wit'out botherin' to greet her. Just walked back to the bed and sat down on the edge of it. Her brows raised when she saw me. The beard on my once hairless face probably tripped her out too. I knew I looked different, but then again, I was.

Kenosha on the other hand looked good. Her chocolate skin was flawless and her thick pink glossy lips were edible. I don't care what else I had on my mind, when I saw her, I wanted to fuck. And it took everything in me to fight my dick from swellin'. She wore a pair of tight ass blue Coogi jeans, and a brown waist length leather jacket. That ass was calling me as she stepped toward me. I was in New York so long I forgot what a sexy-ass DC thoroughbred looked like.

Placing her Louis Vuitton purse on the floor, she knelt and put one hand on my knee. Then she looked into my shades wit'out sayin' a word. She tried to take them off and I tapped her hand. Then I turned away before I addressed her. I couldn't have any *distractions* and distraction was Kenosha's middle name.

"Fuck you doin' here?" I growled.

She sighed.

"I said what the fuck you doin' here, Kenosha? I thought you were comin' tomorrow. And I thought I told you to call first."

Her perfume was the sweetest smell in the room , but I couldn't tell her none of that shit because she fuckin' disrespected my orders even if it had been months since I'd been in the company of a bad bitch of Kenosha's caliber.

"Kelsi…what you still doing here? And why you wearin' shades?" I ignored her. "It's a waste of time beein' here if you ain't find who you lookin' for," she said softly. I wished I never told her what I was here to do. I guess I needed to tell somebody I was gonna kill the niggas responsible for my mother's death. "And look at your face and stuff! You look all *hiiiiigh* and *shiiiiiit*. I thought you was betta den this shit, Kelsi."

"Kenosha…I ain't leavin' 'til I handle my biz. Ain't nobody come out here for no mothafuckin' vacation. So if you tryin' to get me to go back, you might as well kick rocks."

Her head dropped in defeat as she rose to her feet. Then her eyes roamed around the room, as if it were the first time she *really* saw how filthy things were. All of the sheets from the bed were on the floor. My army bag sat on a chair opened, some clothes still in it, the others scattered around the bed. I bought some free weights last month and they did nothin' but add to the mess even though I used them regularly. Everyday I got up early and worked out until the sun went down. I was buildin' up more muscle than ever.

"I ain't tryin' to hear this shit right now," I told her. "I got too much shit to deal wit'."

Kenosha squinted her nose a little and I felt she was gettin' ready to say somethin' else smart. But you wouldn't believe the shit that came out this bitch mouth.

"You been fuckin' somebody else, Kelsi?"

Did I just hear this slut correctly? I'm out here on a mothafuckin' mission and she askin' me if I'm fuckin' somebody. Kenosha not even my girl.

"YOUNG, what the fuck are you talkin' 'bout, Kenosha?" My eyes formed tiny slits as I waited for her answer.

"I mean yo sheets all on the floor and it stiiiinnks in here," she continued rollin' her head before placin' her hands on her hips. "If you ain't been fuckin' it shoooooooo smell like it!"

Please don't tell me this bitch traveled all the way from Maryland to New York just to work my fuckin' nerves. I swear...I ain't got time for this shit. I grabbed her by her arm, lifted her purse from the floor and pushed her ass to the door. As sexy as she was, I ain't tryin' to be bothered.

"Kelsiiiii, you hurtin' meeeeee," she whined as her words drug like always. She was trippin' over her own feet as I shuffled her sideways.

"Kelsiiiii, I'm sorrrrrrrry."

I already had the doorknob in my hand wit' all intentions of throwin' her the fuck out. Wit' the door open, I waited for her to make an exit.

"Kelsiiii, I neeeeed you. Please don't put me out. I drove sooooo far. I'm sorry. I just wanna stay wit' you tonight. Pleeeeaaaaaase, Kelsiiii. I miss you sooooo much."

I had a soft spot for beggin' women. And she knew it.

I released the door and she closed it. Then I looked into

6

her beautiful face and felt like she was bein' real. Maybe she did need me. Or was I playin' victim to the mental power women had over men. It seemed like every woman I let close to me, my mother included, played some sorta game.

She wrapped her arms 'round my waist and pulled me in. She was use to dominatin'. Use to bein' in control. 'Specially in the bedroom. In fact, the last time I hit that shit, she was in *total* control. But I'ma different person now. So what'd I do? Lifted her ass up so that her body was straddlin' mine, and walked her over to the bed. Her eyes widened when she felt her body floatin' in the air. I guess she ain't respect how strong a nigga was 'til now. She threw her arms 'round my neck and placed them lips I been dreamin' 'bout since she walked through the doors on me. A nigga was sweaty and high but she ain't care.

I tossed her body on the mattress. Once on the sheet-less bed, I examined her sexy frame. Her 5'7 inch body moved a few times cuz of the squeaky bedsprings. She jive smiled a lil bit when she saw my devilish grin. Wit'out order, she turned around and wiggled that plump ass out them jeans. On her hands and knees, she rotated her ass so that I could get a good look at the pink center by movin' her panties a lil' to the right. The cherry color thong she wore invited me. I unzippened my fatigues and they dropped over my butter color timbs. Then I took my dick out of my boxers and held it in my hands 'til it grew to complete fullness.

She cooed and begged me to hurry. I ain't want things rushed. It had been a few months since I had a woman and I wanted to take my time.

"You gonna stand over there, or are you gonna come get this pussssssssy?"

I smiled at that sly shit she said out of her mouth. Then I stooped down and ripped her panties off. I changed my mind, tonight I ain't feelin' like makin' love. I wanted to fuck. Straight up! I had a lot of shit on my mind and sex was the best way to get it off.

"That's what I'm talkin' bout, Kelsiii! You not gonna tell me you don't miss this puuusssssy. Show and prove, nigga."

Wit' her waist on the bed and her ass raised high in the air, I slid into her from behind. Slowly. Her mouth opened and she bit her fat pink bottom lip.

"Fuck!" I let out when I was sucked halfway into her tightness.

I was trynna maintain control but Kenosha's pussy was too good. I continued to go in and outta her slowly pullin' her closer. I wanted to see that ass up close. Her face was pressed against the dirty old mattress but she ain't care. We was fuckin' ghetto style. No frills. Just two bodies gettin' it in. I grabbed her closer and pushed all ten inches inside her.

"Oh shiiiiiiit, Kelsi!!! You...you."

"Shut the fuck up!" I was tired of hearin' her mouth.

"I can't...I don't reeeemember you feelin' this good." She stuttered.

Suddenly I snapped. I don't know why. But I pulled my dick out her soaked pussy and fucked her in the ass instead. She tightened up at first as I gave her the *unexpected*. But I wasn't the first nigga who been up in here. I could tell. So she eased up, slightly. I started thinkin' 'bout everything. How much hate I had in my heart. How much I wanted to torture Kyope and Jarvis and how fucked up my life had been ever since they took the only true thorough chick I'd ever known. My moms. Wit' Kenosha still under me, I fucked her rougher. The rougher I got the better it felt. The idea of revenge turned me on even if I was taken it out on the wrong person. I was reckless.

"Ahhhhhh.....shit, I'm bout to bust," I yelled as I released into her warmth clinching her ass tightly.

"Kelsi, please! You hurtin' me."

Her cries woke me out of the zone I was in. But only after I bust my nut. When I let up off of her, she sat up straight, grabbed her legs and backed against the head board. It knocked softly against the wall twice before stoppin'. She was shakin' and I noticed that blood covered the blue mattress and added to the stains already on the bed. I wondered what secrets besides mine this room held.

I couldn't look at her at first, but I could feel her eyes on me. As wrong as I was, I couldn't bring myself to apologize. Apology was a sign of weakness. It meant that your actions, whatever they were, were a mistake. And nothin' I did was a mistake. She wanted to come out here, and she deserved exactly what she got. Fucked!

"You aight?" I managed to say.

"What is wrong with you, Kelsi? Who are you?" she sobbed looking at me strangely.

I ain't answer. I wasn't gonna show her a vulnerable side where there was none.

"Just leave, Kenosha. You shouldn't be here no way. It ain't safe."

Her head dropped and she looked up at me again, naked from the waist down.

Still shaken.

Still scared.

"It's okay. I'll be fine," she wiped her own tears. "I know you gotta lot on your mind right now, Kelsi." She crawled toward me, and grabbed my hand. "Please lay wit' me, Kelsiiiiiii. I'm aight. Really. Pleeeeaaaase. Lay wit' me," she begged.

I wanted to be by myself but I let her stay. Maybe I didn't wanna be alone wit' myself and my thoughts. She turned on her side, away from me and I slid behind her in a spoon fashion. I could feel her tremblin'.

"Kelsiiii, I care 'bout you," she said softly.

"I know." I responded, wit'out emotion.

"I wish you'd let me love you."

"I can't."

MONDAY, 11:31 AM

****

*All I need in this world is a fat pocket and a phat pussy.
You can keep the rest.*

-Jarvis

Larou "Steel" Simmon's funeral was jammed packed and the small church in Harlem had to conduct six services just so everyone could pay their respects. Some sobbed over the loss, while others showed up to be present for yet another fabulous event. Jarvis sat in the back row of the church with Prangsta discussing business. And although he paid for the ceremony, attending felt more like a chore than anything.

"The recipe is still off. Sometimes we get it right, and sometimes we don't," Prangsta said eyeing the huge crowd in front of him. Every now and again he'd use Steel's obituary to fan himself as sweat poured down his face.

"Ya'll niggas stay fuckin' shit up," he looked at him

briefly and shook his head in disgust. He was sick of smelling the foul odor of his unkempt locks. "How hard is it to torture a nigga, write down what he tell you, and put it into action? I mean, must I do everything?"

"We did write down everything, man. But lately we just been off. Plus JoJo been sick so he ain't cookin' no more. For the most part it's just been me and Crane."

"Fuck is wrong wit', JoJo anyway?"

"They say he got that cancer shit and ain't been feelin' right."

"Yeah will he betta die or hurry up back to work foe he get cut the fuck off!"

Jarvis was serious about his business. It wasn't easy becoming a billionaire. In order to corner the market, they needed something that would keep people coming back seconds after they shot up and the average dope wouldn't do it. After word got around that Black Montel, a dealer down south was dominating by manufacturing his own product, Jarvis and Kyope decided to make the trip to Texas. Manufactured dope was the new wave. Black Montel had a white chemistry student on his team who did just that. It wasn't just any dope Black Montel sold. It was so addictive that it had people shooting up within feet of where they copped, just to come back seconds later to cop again.

They tried to reach the white kid and it was impossible. Nobody knew his identity. And getting close to Black Montel proved to be difficult too because his security was top notch. In fact, it took months to win Black Montel's trust and even then, he wasn't willing to give up his recipe. His only offer was to discount his wholesale price since they came prepared to do *big* business. Black Montel's generosity was due primarily to the weight being too small to takeover but large enough to flood New York. He liked to remain in charge.

Black Montel's offer wasn't good enough for Jarvis and Kyope. After a gun show which left twelve of Black Montel's men dead, Jarvis and Kyope managed to throw Black Montel into the trunk of their car and torture him until he told them how he made the dope he called, "Buckle". It was named for curling niggas over after the first pull.

Only after pulling up his toe nails, taping his eyelids back and pouring rubbing alcohol in them, did he talk. He was so determined to die with the information that he endured hours of abuse. Realizing a quick death would be less painful, he finally spoke.

"I'll tell you what you wanna know!" Black Montel cried as alcohol fell into his eyes stinging terribly. "Just please....kill me! I can't take it!"

Jarvis looked at Kyope and smiled at his defeat.

Before killing him, they made sure the recipe was right. Jarvis and Kyope were shocked that dope mixed with a caffeine powder substance could be such a commodity. That was six months ago and now they were two of the richest niggas in America. But with JoJo being unable to cook, lately they were killing more people than they were causing addictions and dope heads were copping elsewhere.

"How ya'll know it ain't workin' right anyway?" Jarvis questioned.

"We been givin' out testers and niggas been droppin' dead. At first it ain't matter cuz word got out that we had the truth. After a while niggas was droppin' like flies and word got out not to fuck wit' us at all."

"You mean in all of New York you can't find one mothafucka that'll try the shit out?"

"You know they'll always be at least one mothafucka. But we not getting' the flow we use to. I mean...we can go to DC and try it there. But 'round New York, it just ain't happenin'. And until we get it right, we short."

"You niggas is worthless!" Jarvis focused on Steel's mother as she wept over the casket. He knew from Steel that she indulged herself every now and again. Her pale white face showed years of dope abuse. He decided to use her as a tester. " Don't cut the dope wit' nothin' 'til it's proper. Just sell it straight up. And then I want you to get JoJo and have him show you how to cook."

"But he in the hospital. He dyin', man."

"You heard me right? Drag his half-dead ass to the lab and have him show you. Cause if my product not right, I'm testin' it on you next."

A surge of fear went through Prangsta.

"And when it's done, we'll rename it "The Crown".

"Why 'The Crown'?" Prangsta asked hesitantly.

"Cuz when they first try it, they'll feel like kings and queens. And then they'll be stripped of all their possessions, startin' wit' they money first."

"I like that," Prangsta smiled trying to get back on his good side.

"Get off my dick and get on top of this project. You got two days. After that I'ma find ya best vein."

MONDAY, 1:00 PM

****

Kelsi ain't the same. He Different. Then again, neither am I.

-Kenosha

The gun shook in my hands as I straddled Kelsi while he slept. The barrel aimed at his head. I wanted to squeeze the trigger so badly I felt sweat forming on my upper lip and forehead. I tried to think of one reason I shouldn't kill him after the way he fucked me last night. Right when I was about to squeeze the trigger, Kelsi moved and saw me over him.

"Bitch, what you-,"

I pulled the trigger! *Bam!* And then I pulled it two more times! *Bam! Bam!* The sound of the blast scared me and I woke up. Wow, what a fucked up ass dream! The bed was wet with my sweat and Kelsi wasn't there.

Sitting up straight on the bed in my panties with my legs

folded against my chest, I still can't get over how disgusting this room is. I walked over to the window to let the New York City air in. Pushing the curtains aside I inhaled the cool breeze and smiled at the slight chill. As I turned around to face the room again, I saw the sun rays light up the dust particles like glitter. This place is beyond filthy.

I decided that today, I would fulfill my duties and work Kelsi harder to murder Jarvis. I'm tired of him wastin' time! Even I knew it didn't take months to murder a mothafucka. If Skully wasn't so concerned about the sentimental value of having Kelsi kill Jarvis instead of me, he'd be dead already cuz I would've done it a long time ago. Shit, I'd kill both of them at the same time!

Let me tell you a little about me. I assisted Skully, my boyfriend...slash sugar daddy...in murdering Kelsi's mother. But Kelsi was told by Skully that Jarvis, his mother's ex-boyfriend from New York did it. And this is all because Jarvis, who happens to be in the drug business with Skully, was stealing from him. I know it gets confusing and sometimes it's even harder for me to understand. So let me reduce it to laymen terms for all you dumb mothafuckas out there. Skully is paying me twenty thousand dollars to see to it that Kelsi settles *his* score. And that's exactly what I intend on doing.

I was just getting ready to put my clothes on and try to find something to do with myself when my cell phone rang. The moment I flipped open the Razr lid and saw Skully's number, I felt a slight pang in my right temple. I hated talking to him sometimes because he wanted everything to his way.

"Hello," I say, as I pull my hair back in a ponytail while resting the phone on my shoulder.

"What the fuck's goin' on, Kenosha?"

"Nothin' yet. He says he's still following them," I told him as I cross my legs in front of me and sit back on the headboard which knocks against the wall. I'm getting real sick of the weak headboard shit. "But he seems motivated enough."

Skully breathed heavily into the phone and said, "Has he told you anything about *when* he plans on killing him?"

Wow. This is a first. Skully is slippin' because he never discusses matters over the phone. I know now that he's desperate so I decide to make my offer again.

"Not really…just that he's not giving up until he handles his biz. But you know what I think. You should just let me handle it. Just show me Jarvis's picture and let me slump his ass."

"No."

I sighed.

"Encourage him, Kenosha. Get into his head! Remind him that his mother is no longer here cuz of Jarvis."

"What you think I been doin'?" I shot back. "Just fuckin' him?"

"Bitch, I will strangle you wit' my bare hands! You hear me?" I Sigh.

"Kenosha…do you hear me?"

"Yeah," I said, as my eyes roll.

"Now if you push him enough, he'll make a move. But you gotta work him though."

The more and more I work for Skully, the more I'm starting to hate his guts. Don't get it twisted, he's paying me good money to be out here dealing wit' this bullshit, but the matter in which he handles affairs is dumb.

"I'll push him, Skully. But you should know he's after Kyope too. I know that ain't in your plan but it's in his."

"Don't worry 'bout that part. He ain't doin' shit 'til he kill Jarvis first, and when he do, you can put a bullet in his head. Can I count on you for that?"

"Do I suck ya dick better than Jordan dunks basketballs?" He laughed. "I got you," I reminded him. "Just let me work my magic."

After I hung up with Skully, I looked around the room again. Something had to give if I was going to hang around here for a few more days. I reached for the old vanilla colored phone by the bed and picked up the receiver to call housekeeping.

"Hello...this is room 316. Is this housekeeping?"

"Yes...what can we do for you?" a woman with a slight African accent asked.

"I'ma need somebody to come clean this room. It looks like it hasn't been cleaned in days."

"But...uh...the last few maids said the guest was adamant about us not entering. I really don't want to go against his wishes."

"Well I'm adamant about ya'll cleaning this bitch. And bring some extra disinfectant too."

When I hung up with her I reached in Kelsi's bag, sniffed some sweatpants and slipped into them after confirming they were clean. Then I called Aunt Grace, Delonte's mother. Delonte was my first cousin, who I was fuckin' on a regular basis. And he just so happen to be fucking Janet, Kelsi's mom too. Don't start trippin'. There are more people fuckin' their first cousins than you realize. I just happen to be one of the ones who don't give a fuck. Hell...I got a friend who was married to her first cousin and didn't even know it. Anyway, Kelsi and Janet murdered Delonte. And since he was Aunt Grace's only son, she started clinging on to me cuz I'm her niece.

"Auntie Grace, its Kenosha."

"Where have you been, girl? I been worried sick! Is everything okay?"

"Yes, auntie. Everything's fine." I slipped into one of Kelsi's fresh white t-shirts at the bottom of his bag. I really should just go to my car and bring my stuff in, but not 'til this fuckin' room is clean.

"When you coming home?"

Home? It was always weird to hear her say that. I hadn't had a home or anything resembling it in my 25 year old life. My family disowned me after I decided *not* to pursue some bullshit ass high paying job wit' the college degree they paid for from Howard University.

I liked the streets. In fact, I loved the streets, and everything in them. Just cuz I talked ghetto doesn't mean I'm one hundred percent ghetto. I put on that ghetto shit for Kelsi. I fluently speak Spanish, French and Russian and could be anything to any man at any time. Kelsi thinks I'm dumb because my words drag when I speak to him. So I become a dumb bitch cuz that's what he needs. Shit, if I wanted to, I could run *and* own a fortune 500 company. I'm a boss bitch! Believe dat!

"I'll be there next week, auntie," I lied.

"Okay. Just call me more. That way I won't worry."

I heard knocks at the door, opened it and saw it was the maid. A petite white woman walked in hesitantly, propping the door open with a stopper.

"Okay, auntie I have to go. Bye." I ended the call before she could contest.

"You called for housekeeping?"

"Yeah…and you betta clean this mothafucka good too." I said reaching in my purse dropping a twenty dollar bill on the bed.

Her eyes lit up as she roamed around the room cleaning up Kelsi's mess. She left thirty minutes later. Then I grabbed the phone book and called a town car to take me around. Believe it or not, this was my first time in New York and everybody told me I had to see Manhattan. So I'ma take some of the cash Skully gave me to burn the stores up.

I ran outside to get my Louis Vuitton luggage from my car and hustled back up the stairs. I hopped in the shower and gave my body a thorough cleaning. I was careful cleaning around my asshole because last night it seemed like Kelsi was banging my shit for points and the opening was still raw.

Once I was done, I smoothed on some Angel body lotion and slipped on my panties. Deciding to look extra-specially-sexy today, I slipped into my Rock & Republic tight fitting blue jeans, a black top with my brown waist length fur and black Maison Martin Margiela boots. My look wasn't complete without my smoky tinted Tom Ford shades. When I was sure I looked stunning, I waited anxiously for my ride.

Moments before leaving, Kelsi opened the door, and I couldn't help but notice the look on his face. He was far from happy. His eyes scanned the clean room as he held onto two white McDonald bags. I remained seated on the bed.

"What the fuck happened?" He walked in and tossed the bags onto the bed.

"Do you mean who was bold enough to clean this nasty bitch?"

He shot daggers at me with his eyes. You woulda thought I shitted on the floor or somethin'. I did this nigga a favor! He needed to be on his knees sucking my toes!

"You had somebody in here? In my personal space?"

"I thought you would like it! It smelled like piss and shit before I had it cleaned."

"I ain't want nobody touchin' my shit! So why you disrespect?" He looked under the bed and pocketed a blunt I didn't even know was there. If I did, I would've smoked that shit just to get calm enough to sit in this mothafucka without throwing up.

"Kelsi, it ain't disrespect. I did you a favor!"

He gave me the look like, *Bitch, I should crush your shit!* He sat on the bed and looked at me seriously. Wipin' his hands over his face, I took notice to his muscles buckling before his hands dropped by his sides. I wanted to fuck him again but after last night, decided against it.

"You gotta hit it, Kenosha. I got a lot of shit on my mind and I'm five seconds from unleashin' on you."

"I was 'bout to leave anyway, Kelsi. I got a car takin' me to Manhattan later. So trust, it ain't even that deep." I shuffled and then stood up.

"I mean you gotta go back home," he replied.

"Kelsi, please. Stop trippin'."

I stood up. And for some reason I became enraged. Who the fuck did he think he was talkin' to? If he woulda smoked Jarvis' ass a long time ago, I wouldn't even be here. So I started laughing.

"Fuck is so funny?"

"You, Kelsi. You sittin' here checkin' me 'bout havin' this raggedy ass room cleaned, when you supposed to be here in your mother's name. If you wanted to just live in a hotel room and hide like a bitch, you coulda did that in Maryland. Sometimes I think you just stupid."

He stood up and I knew I could've stopped there but decided to hammer home.

"Plus I think you scared. Cuz if a nigga woulda merked my mother, I'da dealt wit' that shit wit' the quickness," I giggled throwin' my purse over my shoulder.

He took two steps toward me, reached out wit' his left hand and squeezed my throat.

"If I ever see you again, I'ma kill you. Get the fuck out!" He released me. When a car beeped outside, I rubbed my throat.

"I'm gone, Kelsi," I said as I picked up my purse which had fallen to the floor. "But I sure hope you carry it like that when you see Jarvis. Because I'm not your enemy. You are."

He smirked and instead of leaving before he tried to hurt me, I was determined to know why.

"What's funny?"

"You?" he grinned. "I notice your accent and slang leaves at will. I'm up on your shit. I know you try to act dumb for me. And any bitch who would go through those extremes is not one I want around. Now kick rocks."

Wow! How did he know that? His observation scared me. Still, I managed a smile right before I left the room. But the moment the door was closed behind me, across the parking lot, I saw someone staring at me. It was a dark-skin man in his late thirties and he was sitting in a dark blue Ford. When our eyes met, he grinned devilishly and pulled off. Who was he? And most of all, what did he want with me?

MONDAY, 4:45 PM

****

The prettiest thing I ever seen is green and thin and ain't shit else come close to it since.

–Jarvis

The New York City sidewalk was jumping as women young and old looked at the handsome man who just stepped out of a silver May Bach in style. Even under the winter sky he was hot. Jarvis moved like waves in an ocean as he walked toward the Toys-R-Us in Manhattan. It was his nephew's birthday and he promised to get him a gift for his party which he was already late for. Wearing a pair of blue jeans, a brown corduroy blazer with a black custom made shirt under it, he looked smooth. His five o'clock shadow dressed his brown skin softly. And the prominent mole under his left eye gave him a baby face appeal.

"Look, don't let that nigga go 'til he tell you how he gonna come up wit' all my money. Then follow his ass to it. And if you don't get it by the time I get my sister's kid this gift," he barked into the phone. "Kill his ass no questions asked!"

Before Prangsta could respond, the other line beeped. It was Jarvis's sister who had been pestering him nonstop. Jarvis knew she wanted to know where he was. Had he not been fuckin' one of his boy's girlfriends, he would've gotten the gift earlier and been on time for the party.

"Fuck," he said out loud. "I know her ass gonna trip!" Instead of dealing with her quick lip, he focused back on his conversation with Prangsta. "Like I said, hot that nigga if he don't come up wit' my money. Somebody been fuckin' wit' my shops for the last month and I'm tired of this shit. Niggas gotta be held accountable! And so do you."

"We got it," Prangsta informed trying to convince his boss he could handle whatever duty he gave him. "Ain't no need in even worrin' 'bout it."

"What about my voice makes you think I'm worried, nigga?" Silence. "Exactly...I ain't worried. But *you* betta be if he still alive and my money not found tonight!"

He slammed his RAZR shut and again his sister's home number flashed on the screen. He waited for her to leave a message but she never did. As far as he was concerned, he could do nothing about his lateness. Jarvis was almost inside the store when a bum in a brown trench coat begging for change blocked his path. The derelict looked at him and saw dollar signs.

"Can you help me out, sir?" the dirty white man begged with a silver bent up cup in his hands. "I'm just trynna get something to eat."

"Get a job!" he laughed. "I'm tired of mothafuckas askin' for handouts!" he continued as he pushed him out his way. When the old man dropped to the filthy New York City ground, he kicked him in his gut causing the man to double over. A few onlookers looked at him with hate. And he dared them with his eyes to say something. Nobody did. Once inside the store he realized he never asked Prangsta was the issue with the "Crown" corrected. He decided to call him back while he had time.

MONDAY, 4:55 PM

****

It don't matter who it is. If they got money, then for the moment, they got me too.

-Kenosha

The streets were crazy and I wasn't use to seein' so many people walkin' back and forth at one time. I had so many bags in the back seat of the town car it was difficult to move. I was thinkin' about goin' back to the hotel dumpin' my clothes and ridin' back to Manhattan to hit a few clubs. Then I remembered, Kelsi told me never to come back. There was nothin' more I wanted to do then to ditch his ass but Skully demanded that I smooth things over wit' him. I hated his fuckin' guts but decided I'd suck and fuck him to sleep later. That should make things okay. I was just about to call him when I saw a silver May Bach pull up on the curb next to Toy-R-Us.

"Excuse me, sir, I'd like to go into the Toy store please,"

I said to the cab driver, while my eyes were glued to the money making ride outside.

"We can't park over there," he complained. "We'll get a ticket."

But when I saw this fine ass dude get out, I became anxious. I had to have him and I had to have him now.

"Either pull over or you not gonna get paid!" I threatened. It's mighty funny how he decided to go against the law to suit my needs all of a sudden. I shook my head as I checked my makeup before I got out. When he pulled over behind the May Bach, I reached into my purse. "If you stay here until I return," I said handing him a hundred dollar bill. "There's more where that came from. Besides, my shit's in here and I'll have somebody kill your ass if you try to steal it."

He grunted and took the money but I knew he wasn't going anywhere. Money spoke volumes where words failed.

I hustled into the store before my target got away. My prey was deep in conversation wit' somebody on his phone and that gave me enough time to execute my plan. I couldn't help but take in the brown blazer and Brown & Black Gucci shoes he was wearing. And that mole under his left eye was too cute for words.

I was so gone I stepped on a kid's toe and she wailed in pain. I pushed her dumb ass out my way quick. I was fixated on Mr. May Bach. So when I saw him grab a Playstation 3 game system and move toward the counter, I moved with him. Realizing I didn't have anything to buy, I grabbed a video game for Kelsi. I didn't realize it was the *Adventures of Strawberry Shortcake* until after I got to the counter. The moment I hit the line, I stepped close to him so that he could smell my scent. I wore the most expensive shit and today I was wearing, *Michael Kors* on top of my *Angel* body lotion. The Combination of the two fragrances was lethal.

"Looks like you ain't gonna pick up no habit after all," he laughed, holding his phone to his ear. "I know you happy 'bout that shit cuz I was serious 'bout usin' your veins." He paused for a while and I coughed loudly trying to get his attention. When he didn't turn around quick enough, I lightly pushed my titties up against his back like people behind me were pushing causing our bodies to connect.

"Oh, I'm sorry," I lied looking behind me at no one. "I'm so clumsy." He looked back at me and smiled.

"Look, nigga. Get that otha shit taken care of and get at me later. Gone." He placed the phone in the clip on his hip and gave me the once over. Everything was in order. I noticed immediately that he was a boss who liked to be in charge. "Strawberry Shortcake huh?" he said as he looked down at the game I was carrying. He pushed the PS3 game system toward the clerk. With one person before him I had to act quickly.

"It takes work tryin' to be this sweet. I have to practice all the time."

And then he said, "I hear you. But when you gonna have time to play a game since you comin' wit a real nigga?"

He moved fast! I've dealt wit' confident men in my day but none as presumptuous as he. But I liked it. I liked it a lot! He made my work easier.

"I guess I gotta play wit' my game *after* I play wit' you." He winked, added my game to his pile and paid for our purchases. We made our way past a few customers and out the door.

"Here you go, man," he said throwin' four C-Notes on a bum who was lying on the ground outside of the store. "Get yourself somethin' to eat." The bum took the cash but appeared be frightened as he collected the money.

"That was nice," I told him. Personally I ain't think the bum deserved shit. If a bad bitch like me had to work, so did this washed up ass bum!

"It's nothin'," he advised as his black driver opened the door to the most beautiful-ist silver May Bach I ever saw in my life! "I do what I can. Money ain't shit but paper." He boasted. I was so captivated that I was about to slide inside the car without my things.

"My bags are still in that town car," I said worriedly looking back at my driver. He parked behind us.

"I got you," he said as he moved in the cab's direction. "You just get your fine ass in the car." I smiled and obeyed. Damn I love his style! He smooth as shit!!

He walked back to the cab and paid his fee. He must've paid the cab driver better than I would have because his scowl was instantly replaced with a huge smile.

"I see you got enough stuff," he winked sliding into the seat next to me. He placed my bags in the seat in front of us.

"Them little-bitty bags? That ain't nothin' compared to the money you gonna spend on me," I promised.

"And what makes you think I'ma spend anything on you?" he smirked.

"You already did," I said referring to the cab driver and the game he purchased in the store. "I know what kind of man you are. You only make smart investments and I'm as smart as they come."

"I like your style," he winked. "You ready to roll?

I didn't respond right away, just inhaled his cologne. A man with money made me weak.

"Of course I'm ready," I blushed. "But do you always take strangers with you everywhere you go?"

"Do you always take rides wit' strangers?" He didn't wait for my response. "Take me to Kecia's!" he yelled to the driver. "I know she trippin' hard by now."

I wondered who Kecia was but didn't bother asking. She had to be family if he was taking me around her. And as long as the bitch didn't trip when I walked through the door wit' him, everything was cool.

"You okay?" he asked with his cool melodic voice. "You want anything to drink?" While he spoke, I focused on his lips...then that mole. Damn he was fine.

I could always get a feel for what a man wanted once in his presence. That has been my gift from day one. Like right now, I know this man likes control and a challenge. From the moment he told me that I was comin' wit' him, 'til the time he paid for my purchases, his actions made it clear.

"Not a problem, sir," the driver said as we floated from the park position. "I'll get us to your sister's house in no time," he continued, maneuvering in the busy traffic.

"I didn't get your name?" I remembered.

"Don't you think askin' my name right now is a lil' late?"

"Better late than never."

"Jay.", he smiled. "For now, just call me Jay."

"Well, Jay, I'm Kay. But you can call me whatever you like. And I mean that."

"I guess we know all we need to 'bout one another."

"I guess so," I giggled crossin' my legs and runnin' my hand down my thigh.

He wrapped his arm around the back of my seat and stared at me. He let me know without words the plans he had for my body. And depending on how he acted, I might be willin' to oblige. We were having light conversation when his phone began to vibrate.

"Hold on," he said staring into my eyes. "It's my sis. I gotta tell her I'm on my way now before she keeps blowin' my shit up."

"Go 'head," I said softly.

I remained silent and imagined how our evening would begin and end. It would *probably* start with me on top of him riding his dick and end with him screaming my name. As thoughts of sex flooded my mind, he undressed me with his eyes. I was still in a daydream until I saw the look on his face. Something changed as quickly as flippin' a light switch from on to off.

"What you say?" he asked the caller on the phone.

Silence. I desperately tried to ear hustle but whoever he was speaking to spoke loud enough for only Jay to hear.

"I'm on my way but if somethin' happens to my family, I'ma find out who this is and kill you. That's a promise!"

"Nigga, you ain't doin' shit!" the person yelled on the phone. The voice sounded male and I was sure it wasn't his sister like he originally thought. "Just get the fuck over here and bring my cash! Or this bitch and her son dies!" I heard that. Clearly. And the grin on my face was wiped clean. Suddenly I began to realize I met my new friend at the wrong time. And all I could think about was...*Damn*.

MONDAY, 7:22 PM

****

Real men don't say they are. It just is.

-Kelsi

Tonight was the night and one of two things was goin' pop off. Either I'd conquer what I came to conquer, or I'd kill one of 'em, lay low, then hit the other one later. I played this event out over and over in my head, so I knew it would work. It had to. There wasn't shit left to do 'cept execute my plan. My plan was simple. Stop the cash flow they received from their operation. Pitch Jarvis and Kyope against each other, and kill 'em both...slowly.

Wave's, a strip club in Harlem was almost packed and I could tell most of the people inside already knew each other. A few dudes moved freely from table to table politicin', while strippers circled them lookin' for the most vulnerable and drunk prey. In the background T.I's, *"Watch What You Say To Me"*, blasted on the speakers and it put me in the mood for what had to be done.

I got there early so I could sit in my normal spot, a few seats over from the VIP section where Kyope and his crew normally chillled. Jarvis *never* came to the spot wit' him. My foot tapped against the grungy floor as I waited for the moment they'd arrive. To waste time, I focused on the baddest strippers in New York as they hopped on poles like monkeys on a tree.

Orgasmic, my partner in crime, and one of the dancers nodded to me acknowledgin' that she was prepared to help me carry out my plans. Although I ain't know much about her and she ain't know much 'bout me, I knew she was a ride or die chick. She ain't ask a lot a questions. I sold her a fake dream and purpose and she bought that shit, hook, line and sink. In her mind, I was tryin' to get put on with Kyope's drug organization and I needed her to do it. I knew even less about her. But before I appealed to her, I did know she was preparin' to quit Waves after gettin' into it wit' one of her co-strippers. The bad thing about it was, I knew more 'bout why she got into the altercation than she did.

A month ago I went to Waves. I knew from my research that every Tuesday and Friday, Kyope and his squad would be there. After 'bout a hour of chillin' I saw Orgasmic come out the dressin' room screamin'.

"Jewels, you stole my money, bitch!" Jewels is a tall dark skin stripper who was overprotective of a large green leather purse she carried 'round like it was a third titty.

"Bitch, I ain't steal shit! I got my own cash!"

"Then why you steal mine?!"

"If you felt I was a thief, you shoulda got another money collector while your fat ass was bouncin' 'round on stage! Cuz everything in my bag," she said tapping it twice. "I earned. And if you don't get outta my face I'ma beat your shit in," she said pointin' in Orgasmic's face. Everybody laughed which encouraged Jewels even more. "Sounds to me like you not hot as you thought you was redbone," Jewels continued. Jewels and her stripper friends continued to laugh and instigate the situation.

"I'm betta than you, you ugly black, bitch!"

"Please! You wish you could get rained on as much as I do when I step on the stage!" Jewels boasted.

"Bitch, I ain't tryin' to hear that shit! Ya'll think just cuz I'm from Atlanta that ya'll can take advantage of me, but that ain't goin' happen! I'll wreck anybody in here...by...myself! I don't give a fuck who it is or how many of ya'll it is!"

"Don't do this, O," Jelly, one of the oldest strippers in the club said. She was the only one that O conversed with. And just like O, she couldn't stand Jewels. They called her Jelly cuz everything on her body shook. Gut included.

"Naw, Jelly...this, bitch got me fucked up!" Orgasmic screamed pushing Jelly out of the way. "And I'm 'bout to show her how we get down in the 'A'!"

Orgasmic walked up to her and pushed Jewels back toward the bar. And even though Jewels had about a foot on her 4 foot 9 inch frame, O ain't care. I had to give O her props 'til out of the blue Jewel came down on her face with a drink glass from the bar O's eyes widened as she felt the damage to her face once it slit a little.

"Bitch, you really do got me fucked up!" O screamed.

Wit'out delay O wailed on Jewels. I guess she felt she wasn't doin' enough damage, cuz she pulled a stun gun out her purse and tazed that bitch several times in the face and neck. The other ho's rushed to the scene throwin' Orgasmic's small body through the air and on top of some wooden chairs. Jelly tried to stop O from gettin' back up but she was on a mission. Her small frame allowed her to move quickly. They wasn't time enough for her and she couldn't be stopped. Part of me wanted her to get away so I could see how lil youngin' wrecked.

A few niggas watched but ain't none of them help. I had

my reasons for not gettin' out my seat too. I wanted O to be mad enough to do what I needed done. I peeped her long enough to know that stealin' tips would not be tolerated and off limits.

"I'm 'bout to kick your ass, bitch!" O screamed.

"Bring it on!" Jewels yelled raisin' her ashy fists in the air.

Not backin' down, O kicked off her classic stripper glass heels and ran toward Jewels. Jewels not expectin' her to get up as quickly as she did, had her back turned as she picked up her bag from the floor. She slept on lil' shawty and had her guards down. She paid for that mistake too.

Huddled in a group wit' some other strippers, Jewels laughed 'bout how she got out on O. They all stuck together and I could tell O wit' her country accent felt out of place. But my jaw hit the floor when I saw O leap onto Jewels back like a human book bag. Wit' her fingers in Jewels' eyes, she pressed into the sockets 'til blood was drawn. Only when Jewels begged her to stop, did she slide off. And even then she ain't stop hittin' her in the back of the neck. The shit was hilarious!

Wit' bare feet, O pulled on Jewels' red thong. The niggas was drunk in the background cheerin' her on. But what I saw next made me choke on my drink. Once O got Jewels thong off, a dick fell from between Jewels legs. The entire club went silent. That would explain why Jewels never removed her thong in the few months I been comin' to the club. I ain't think much about it cuz it's ass was so huge, I let it slide. Now I felt like bringin' the sun down on this bitch. I would have if I ever beat my dick to her image when I was alone. Luckily for her I didn't.

"Now niggas know what's *really* up wit' you, bitch," O said, slappin' his loose dick against his thigh wit' her hand. "Ya'll can have this dirty ass club! I'm outta here."

Jewels stood silent and embarrassed, later runnin' in the back wit' his friends followin'. O gathered her things and exited the club.

That's when I followed. Walkin' barefoot on the sidewalk, O rustled to get one shoe on and then the other. Her glass slippers clicked against the sidewalk as she talked to herself.

"Fuck this place! I ain't dealin' wit' this shit no more!" She cried wavin' her arms. "I ain't gotta be here! I'm betta than all this shit!"

"Can I talk to you for a moment?" I questioned walkin' cautiously a few feet behind.

"No!" she responded not even takin' the time to look at me. "I'm sick of this shit. Get one of them otha bitches to fuck you cuz I don't get it in like that anyway."

"Let me take you home!" I told her.

"I just told you it ain't that kinda party wit' me," she removed a sweater from the large silver beach purse she kept on her shoulder. Still she hadn't looked my way.

"Hold up, Shawty," I called out again. This time my voice was more authoritative. "I need to rap to you!"

She turned around saw it was me and smiled. I knew she had been tryin' to holla at me ever since I showed up at the club...but I brushed her off. It wasn't 'bout sex wit' me even though I would've fucked her a long time ago. Shawty was bad as shit. I was on a mission and needed things to be done in my time. And now it *was* time. She stopped in her tracks and walked toward me. I did the same.

"I saw what happened back there and I'm sorry. That's fucked up how she or he did you. You aight?"

"I'm good. Them bitches got me fucked up though," she said loudly as if she wanted them to come out again so she could fight. "I'm from the south and we don't play that bullshit. It's cool though," she shrugged her shoulders tryin' to be tough, while she tried to get a look at the cut on her face in the store window. "I don't need that spot no more anyway. I'm just mad cuz she got me for my rent money!"

"I feel you. But since you leavin' here anyway, might as

well make some dough first."

Silence.

"Make some dough wit' who?"

"Me?"

She laughed and said, "Where your stripper outfit at? In your back pocket?"

"Don't get smacked, Shawty," I frowned. I had to put her in her place.

She cleared her throat and said, "Well how you gonna make money wit' me then? Cuz in case you ain't noticed, I'm a dancer. And I do 'aight by myself."

"For starters...I'll pay you. There's more than one way to make cash. You ain't always gotta dance on stage. I'll give you more than you was gettin' paid in there for one night."

"For doin' what? I don't want or need no pimp."

"I ain't talkin' 'bout trickin'," I assured her.

"Well what I gotta do and how much you gonna give me?"

"It depends on how much you willin' to help me. Can we go somewhere and talk privately?" She looked me over tryin' to detect any sign of me being crazy. She couldn't see it even though it was there. I smiled and grabbed her hand. She smiled back. "Come on. Just gimme a few minutes of your time baby girl. If you ain't feelin' it, you can say no and be on your way. Deal?"

She shook my hand. We stepped off. Together. We went to a small lounge a few blocks down that served food. I told her what I needed and what I was willin' to pay. She looked scared at first but later agreed.

"Are you sure this'll work?" She pushed her food aside. Her appetite was lost. "I heard stories from the other strippers 'bout how dangerous they are."

"I ain't gonna let nothin' happen to you," I said, lookin' into her eyes. "Trust me."

She smiled again and I knew I had her. Finally I would be

able to get her to do what I needed. What was fucked up was that some of the money I would pay her wit' would be her own. I paid Jelly, her so-called friend, to clip her money while she was on stage. Jewels ain't have nothin' to do wit' that shit. So what it may've been wrong. I needed this chick's help. Luckily for me it ain't cost much.

MONDAY, 8:15 PM

****

Sometimes havin' family can make you soft, and I'm as hard as they come.

-Jarvis

The night air was cool as they walked up to Jarvis's sister's home. At first he was going to drop Kenosha off but she refused saying she'd rather stay by his side. And because he knew that she was aware that nothing positive would happen if she stayed, that made him like her even more. The small green house in Queens looked peaceful under the night sky, but Jarvis was no fool. There was nothing close to peace inside. Still, he entered using his spare key and Kenosha stayed close on his heels.

The door creaked as Jarvis pushed it open. The television was on low yet he could hear Mary J. Blige's melodic voice coming from its speakers. Directly across from the door sat his family, bound and gagged. And when he looked at his sister's face, he saw her tears dried on her face while his nephew sat visibly shaken. The door closed softly behind them as he focused on the strangers standing on each side of the couch.

"You must be the *man!*" a tall, half burned dark skin man laughed. "When you didn't come, I was startin' to believe all that shit they said 'bout you."

"And what's that?" Jarvis asked flatly.

"You know. That you don't give a fuck 'bout nobody but yourself!"

Jarvis ignored the comment and fixed his eyes on his sister again and the young man who was standing behind the couch over his nephew. The duct tape was bound tightly around their mouths.

"Did you bring my money?" the older stranger asked, stopping his stare.

Jarvis nodded yes and tossed the navy blue duffle bag he had in the middle of the floor. Kenosha eyed the bag wondering if money was really inside. She'd been with him from the moment he got the call and was pretty sure it wasn't. She did witness him stuffing the bag with some contents in the back of his trunk, while he spoke on the phone.

"Everything you asked for and deserve is right there," Jarvis said, coldly, pointing to the bag.

"Deserve huh?"

Jarvis smirked.

"Pick it up and open it," the burnt man said to his accomplice. The younger man was much shorter with light skin. Having the same eyes, despite their physical differences, it was apparent they were related.

"Okay," he said hustling from behind the sofa to grab the bag. When the bag was opened, the young man's mouth dropped in fear when he saw a bag full of newspaper. He lifted the bag from the floor and showed the older man.

"What is it?" He asked, seeing the boy's expression then

snatching the bag.

"Paper?" he mumbled.

"What?"

"It's paper, dad." He said grabbing a fistful and showing him.

With rage in his eyes, the man shot Jarvis an evil stare. Kenosha backed up against the front door attempting to get out of the way.

"Do you realize what you just did?"

Jarvis's sister wept. She knew her brother could be stingy but would've never thought he'd take things so far considering their lives were on the line. Jarvis reached behind his back slowly lifting up his shirt. The man was so disturbed at Jarvis's lack of respect that he hadn't noticed his small action. But when he did, Jarvis pulled his weapon and aimed. The burnt man placed his arm around his sister's throat and hoisted her up off the sofa, cutting off most of her air circulation.

"Put the fuckin' gun down before I kill her!" Kecia clawed at the man's forearm but it didn't lessen his grip.

"Who you workin' for?" Jarvis asked ignoring his threat.

"You ain't askin' no fuckin' questions!" he pointed his finger at himself. "I am!" the man yelled, as sprinkles of spit touched his sister's nose. He tightened the grip around her throat, causing her face to turn red. "Who you think you fuckin' wit'?"

"I asked you a question, mothafucka! Who you workin' for?" He took one step closer to the stranger. "Is it Koni?" He took another step. "Or is it D-9?"

Jarvis had wronged so many, that he wasn't sure who was after him. And the only reason he picked Koni was because he fucked his wife then got her strung out on cocaine a few years back.

"You shouldn't fuck so many people outta they money." The man said hysterically. Jarvis could tell he was trying to pump himself up to put in work. "Now either you get me my money....or I'ma slump your family."

Jarvis with his hammer still aimed, smiled. Then he pulled the trigger hitting his sister in the middle of her forehead. When he shot her, he aimed the barrel at the stranger. In disbelief, the stranger allowed her limp body to fall on the floor. He took a few steps back from her body, staring in horror. When he looked at Jarvis, he had a smile on his face.

"You crazy!" the man exclaimed. "You fuckin' crazy!"

While he was talking, Prangsta and Spikes came rushing upstairs from the basement. He didn't know that Kecia had a small door which led from outside in the laundry room. It was obvious he was an amateur. Their abrupt entry startled the stranger causing him to mistakenly drop his weapon. The moment Prangsta and Spikes saw Keicia's body spread out on the floor they violently grabbed the two from behind.

"You want me to murder his ass?" Prangsta asked, as he wrapped his arm around his throat. Spikes grabbed the younger man. "Let me do it, man!" Kenosha was stunned because she was certain Jarvis killed his sister on purpose.

"Not yet," he eyed his nephew who was visibly distraught.

Jarvis walked up to the burnt man as Prangsta maintained the grip around his neck.

"I'm gonna ask you again," he said softly. "Who sent you?" The man was silent at first but then his demeanor changed. It was evident that he was petrified.

"I don't know his name. He gave me the lick and said he'd meet me for his five percent." That bothered Jarvis. He hated the idea of someone trying to play him.

"What did he look like?"

"He was tall, dark skin and older. Maybe 'bout forty. That's all I know! On my mother! I wasn't gonna hurt your family, man. I'm just tryin' to feed my seed. That's it!"

"Hey, Jarvis...Ice said that the dude who stuck him up

looked the same way."

Jarvis? Kenosha thought. *It can't be!* Her mind was on speed as she focused on his features. She could see why Janet got with him.

"You had to use my name, huh?" Jarvis asked disgusted with his lack of ethics.

"Sorry, man. I figured we was gonna hot they asses anyway." Jarvis shook his head.

"Go 'head, nigga."

Prangsta proceeded cautiously and said, "He was talkin' to some dude who said on his mother, he was gonna keep stickin' you until he takes back everythin' you took from him. It may be the same dude who keeps robbin' our shops."

"I can't believe one nigga causin' all these problems!" Jarvis said, frustrated as he took his right hand and placed it on top of his head. It seemed a little inappropriate to disgust business over his sister's dead body but that was the nature of the man. "But that's what it sounds like." Jarvis mind raced. *Who the fuck is this nigga?* Jarvis looked back at Kenosha who appeared calm despite being slightly nervous. Then he looked at Prangsta and said, "Kill 'em both."

Prangsta grabbed the man and he and Spikes were both on their way down the stairs when the stranger said to Jarvis, "Can I ask you a question before I die?"

"No fuck that shit!" Prangsta yelled pushing him toward the basement.

"Hold up...I never deny a dead man his final wish," Jarvis interrupted. Prangsta turned the man around so that he could look Jarvis in his eyes. His son could be heard weeping at his fate was soon to come. "What you wanna know?"

"Did you kill your sister on purpose?"

It was silent as Jarvis took a few moments before answering his question. Prangsta and Spikes gave one another befuddled looks.

After a few minutes of silence Jarvis said, "What you think?"

After his response Prangsta and Spikes took both men downstairs and killed them. Jarvis grabbed his nephew and walked out the door with Kenosha.

MONDAY, 9:15 PM

****

Who need a job when ya got a rich nigga?

-Kenosha

Drivin' through the streets of Brooklyn changed what I originally thought. That all projects was the same. There was something about Marcy Projects that pulled my breath. The big red buildings appeared larger than life under the night sky and people seemed to be possessed by its power.

"Gimme a sec, Kay," Jarvis said without waiting on my response.

He grabbed his nephew's hand and they exited the May Bach. The child looked about ten years old. Jarvis appeared unnerved that he'd just killed his mother, and that his nephew was still physically and mentally shaken. Once outside the car, he stooped down and gave the little dude orders I couldn't hear. What could he possibly have wanted from a child at a time like this? When Jarvis walked back to the car, without his nephew, I figured I'd get my answer. But where was his nephew going?

"You aight?" He asked.

I nodded yes as I watched his nephew disappear within the darkness of the buildings. Although he asked me a question, I could tell he cared less about my reply. And then I remembered. He was Jarvis. *Kill him now and put this all behind you.* I thought as I stared at the back of his head while he looked out of the window. My mind went into overdrive until Jarvis turned away from the window and looked me in my eyes.

"You know I fucks wit' you right?"

"I guess…uh…why you say that?"

"I just do." Silence. "I can tell from the gate you not a stranger to this shit. Right?" He sat back in the seat and appeared to be reading me. I didn't answer. I didn't know what to say. "I'm serious. Any other bitch woulda been complainin' or askin' to go home. You different. Why you different, Kay?"

"I'm no different than any other girl," I lied.

"Who the fuck are you?" he asked flatly. His demeanor went from cold to hot. "The shit you witnessed tonight shoulda had you vexed. Am I gonna have to kill you? Did somebody send you to get to me?" Why would he suddenly ask me who was I? Could he hear my thoughts? Before I could give him a response he chuckled loudly. "I'm just fuckin' wit' you," he boasted. "You should've seen the look on your face, though! You probably thinkin' *"This nigga crazy as shit"*.

I was. But…I gave no response.

"Trust me," he continued. "I can spot a snake. And if you were out to get me, you would've been dead a long time ago." His statement sounded like a promise. "And there's no need in me tellin' you not to disgust what you saw tonight with anyone. You already know the consequences that could carry."

"It was none of my business." I told him. He smiled. I didn't.

His nephew was on his way back when Prangsta pulled up in a white Ford pick-up truck and got inside the May Bach. Before chatting with Prangsta, his nephew got in and handed him a wad of money. He looked sad.

"That's all he had. He said D9 got the rest." His nephew muttered.

Jarvis looked frustrated.

"Good job, lil man," He rubbed his head. "And don't worry 'bout that shit back at your crib. You gon' be good now. I'ma take care of you. Believe that."

A tear fell from the child's eye.

While they talked, Prangsta stared. I could tell he was trying to figure me out and I wanted him *not* to waste his ugly time. The driver suddenly pulled off.

"Everything taken care of," Prangsta looked at me one last time. He was talking to Jarvis.

"Good. Don't tell nobody the details of tonight, especially Kyope."

Prangsta nodded.

"So boss...what's up wit Lil' Brian? Why he go into Marcy?"

"To get my money," he snickered. "They may want my life but they not gonna fuck wit' a kid."

I'm not gonna lie, puttin' the kid into harm's way rubbed me wrong.

We made a few stops and Jarvis did other shit that amazed me. Apparently he was looking for someone who owed him money. And when he couldn't find him, he found the person's mother instead.

"There his mother go," Prangsta said pointing at a woman wrestlin' wit' two grocery bags in her hands. She had just gotten off the public bus. "Maybe she can tell us where he at."

Jarvis instructed the driver to pull over as he hopped out the car. I remained seated wit' a perfect view from the inside. The woman was startled at first when she heard someone call out to her, but smiled having seen Jarvis' face. She must've trusted him. But like a woman who knows her rapist, her expression immediately changed to terror.

Without warning he back handed the elderly woman to the ground and her blue knit hat flew off exposing her long beautiful gray hair. Then he choked her in the middle of the yard with witnesses watching.

"Where your son, bitch?!" he yelled, manhandling her.

"I...don't know where he is! What's wrong?"

"Then where is that fuckin' nephew of yours?!" He continued, maintaining the hold.

"Please...you're hurting me," she said softly. Her voice was growing faint.

I looked at the driver who shook his head in disgust and then focused back on Jarvis. His nephew who had seen enough horror for the day lie quietly in the back seat.

"Well you make sure you tell both of them this. If they don't have my money by tomorrow night, I'ma come back here and beat your ass everyday 'til my debt is paid. You hear me?" He smacked her again. Blood escaped her cut lips. "You betta make sure you tell em! Every fuckin' day!"

He released his hold and rummaged through her pockets. He smiled when he found a little cash. Afterwards he grabbed two pieces of fruit from the bag. A few of the neighborhood dealers looked at him with hate but not one of them helped her out.

"What? Ya'll want some of me too?" he asked with his arms raised. The yard fell silent. "I said do anyone of you mothafuckas want it wit' me?!" He pointed to himself. Silence. "I run New York and everybody in it! Nobody fucks wit' me or my money!"

Prangsta stayed by his side while he ranted and raved. And when Jarvis was done, he said something to Prangsta and he came back to get the kid. Together, they walked off.

Once back inside the car Jarvis' face was still distorted until he closed the door and looked at me. He must've told Prangsta to roll and take his nephew with him.

"Take me back to my crib," he told the driver before looking at me. "Hungry?"

I nodded yes.

"Doby, take us to Manhattan instead. My lady hungry back here." He handed me one of the two apples he'd taken from the old woman. "You my lady right?" he asked stroking my leg harder. His question was odd and childlike but I had become aware of his weaknesses. Women.

"I don't know…what you gonna do to convince me to be your lady? I mean, you hardly even know me."

"All you need to know is this…I run New York and everybody in it. And if you by my side, you can have whateva you want. Can you handle that?"

"I can handle it."

"You gonna be happy you said that," he winked. "You gonna spend the rest of *your* life with me." The rest of *my* life? I thought. Why not *ours*? Everything in me told me I should leave, and cut him off but I couldn't. He was a total stranger who committed enough crimes in front of me today to get him life. He wasn't stable. He wasn't normal. Yet I found him interesting and couldn't leave.

"We'll see," I told him. "We'll see."

And when I looked away from him to glance through my window, I saw that same car that had been sitting outside of the hotel earlier wit' the same man inside. I was so nervous my stomach began to churn. I looked away. Looked back. And he was gone.

Who was he?!

MONDAY, 9:33 PM

****

Just cuz my actions are slow don't mean I ain't quick.

-Kelsi

When Kyope and his crew got in, I took a deep breath and sat back into the old wooden chair. The two loud mouth niggas on my left were drowned out. And the music which at first kept me company, I could no longer hear. I was enveloped in silence. Unconsciously…I grabbed the glass which held the remnants of my drink and slid it back and forth on the table. I had to do somethin'. Because what I really wanted to do was wrap my hands 'round Kyope's throat. But everything in time. My time.

I couldn't believe after all the months of plannin', shit was finally gettin' ready to pop off. The club was jumpin' as usual. Niggas removed they rings and acted like they was single just to get a better lap dance from the baddest stripper's in New York. Big Kuntry's, *The Baddest* blared from the speakers as the dancers did what they did best. Seduce. I had my mind on one thing. Murder.

The only thing 'bout my plan was if Kyope *really* knew my mother outside of her being just Jarvis's girl, he'd recognize me. Even with the shades I never took off. From what she told me, Jarvis and Kyope were always together. Outside of bein' a little older, my features were the exact same. I did allow time to grow a beard which is one of the reasons why I didn't approach him right away. My only flaw was the tattoo I had on my arm. I got it after my moms died. It read, *Kelsi AKA K-Man loves you Ma. RIP.* K-Man was the nickname she gave me which I use to hate. What I wouldn't give to hear her say it now.

As always, Kyope's crew was loud. I counted four of them. Kyope ain't say much, but his squad was on some other shit. I sat quietly in the table next to them. I could hear every word they said...*clearly.*

"I'm 'bout to tell you what happened again cuz I know you don't believe me," Prangsta said, after they all took they seats. He had on a heavy red jacket even though the weather outside ain't call for all that shit. I'm pretty sure he was concealin' a weapon. "I went to this club a few months back and these two bitches asked me over to the bar. So I goes ova and we get to drinkin'...and they start talkin' 'bout all the shit they wanna do to me. You shoulda heard em'!"

"Hold up," Spikes, another one of Kyope's crew members interrupted. He rubbed his chin and looked up at the ceilin' briefly. "Did they start stroking your dick at the bar and offer to take you to the bathroom to fuck?" he questioned Prangsta.

"Yeah," Prangsta nodded, excitedly. "How you know? I told you this story already?" They all looked at each other and exchanged dialogue with they eyes. Once again he was swag jackin'.

"Nigga you ain't tell me that story. I told *you* that story! Always stealin' other niggas lives cuz ya own shit too borin'."

They all laughed while Prangsta did his best to conceal his embarrassment.

I learned from my surveillance that Prangsta was the muscle but also a liar. He would tell stories other people told him like he actually lived it. The thing about it was, he really believed half of the shit he said. The nigga is pathetic. But outta all of 'em, he was the one I had to worry 'bout. Not cuz he was vicious but cuz he acted on impulse.

"That shit ain't happen to you! It happened to me!" Prangsta responded.

"Nigga, stop lyin'," Kyope laughed. "If it wasn't you, it wasn't you."

"I'm serious, man! That shit *did* happen to me! Straight up!" Prangsta put his right hand on his heart and placed the other hand in the air like he was bein' sworn in or some shit. They all busted out in laughter and his hands fell to his lap in defeat.

"Put ya dumb ass hand down! Ain't no need in talkin' 'bout it no more. You takin' lives! Simple as that," Spikes sat back in his seat and folded his arms.

They all laughed harder.

Spikes and Prangsta stayed goin' at it. Like brothers. Tall with deep dark skin, Spikes reminded me of Stringer Bell from the show, *The Wire*. From what I could gather, Kyope trusted him more cuz on more than one occasion, he and Kyope would leave the others to talk privately.

"Ya'll laughin'," Spikes continued. "But this nigga be really believin' half the shit he tell us." The laughter softened and Kyope focused on Spikes.

"You laughin', Spikes, but how come none of us have *ever* seen you wit' no certified bitch? You act like you don't fuck wit' pussy, I ain't even sure if that story Prangsta tried to jack was really *your* story." They all cosigned and waited for his answer.

"You don't see me wit' none cuz ain't no certified bitches out here, slim. So *when* and *if* you do see me wit' one, best believe she'll be under lock and key," Spikes said as the waitress came over bringin' they usual drinks.

"You sure that's it?" Kyope questioned. "Cuz I can't have not botty-boy on my team."

"Whateva, man. Just cuz I ain't trippin' off females don't mean I don't love pussy. I probably get more pussy than all you mothafuckas put togetha! I just don't brag on mine all the time."

I was still listenin' 'til "O" walked up to me. She was wearin' a red lace bodysuit and every curve of her body was revealed.

"What time you want me to do it, Aven?" Orgasmic asked, runnin' her tongue over her lips. She sat on me, pretendin' to give me a lap dance so that our conversation wouldn't look suspicious.

Wit' the thickness of her ass in my lap, I whispered, "Do it now."

Her head turned slightly so she could see me. The smell of weed and perfume lingered in the air next to her. She must've smoked the dro I gave her earlier so she could relax. I was happy cause this bitch tried to bail out on me three times since our agreement. After I told her how much it would mean to me, she agreed to go through with it. Her eyes told me she hoped after-wards, I'd be wit her.

"Aven…don't worry, I'm not gonna let you down," she said softly windin' her hips in my lap harder.

I told her my name was Aven. It was sure for Avenge.

"I ain't worried. I know you got me on this. But I'ma need you to do it in the next five minutes," I told her as she start-ed windin' like she was puttin' in work for real. "You remember what you 'sposed to do, right?"

"Yep. Cuz after this, I'm goin' back to Atlanta. Ain't nothin' here for me no way but trouble. Just make sure you give me my money."

I knew O wasn't doin' this for the two thousand dollars I

promised her after it was done. She was doin' it for me. I don't know what brought her up from Atlanta, cuz I never asked, but I knew strippin' wasn't in her blood. I neva asked too many questions 'bout her past cuz I ain't want her askin' me shit 'bout mine.

"Okay...let me get ready." She eased off me *just* before I got hard. I slid her a $20 bill to make the fake lap dance appear legit. "I gotta smoke again," she said before she disappeared into the thickness of the club. When she was gone, I focused back on my target. Kyope had just gotten off a call and appeared vexed. I listened closer to what he was sayin'.

"Where, Jarvis at?" Kyope questioned his men, placin' his phone back on his hip. "A lot of shit been happenin' in the past few months and I'm sick of excuses."

"He wit' that bad ass bitch I was tellin' you 'bout earlier. He ain't comin' out tonight, Kyope. You know wit' that shit that just happened wit' his sister." Prangsta told him. Kyope sipped on his drink and I could tell he was tryin' to calm down.

"You want anotha one?" The waitress asked, Kyope. He said no and then she asked Crane.

Crane was also muscle but he had a flaw. He was deaf. When I asked O how it happened, she said she didn't know much about him. Just that he was shot in one ear and the bullet went out the other. Although he was deaf, he could read lips. He was nicknamed Crane cuz he always wore a navy blue one piece uniform and a navy blue hat. The work uniform came from *Crane Construction* company, the place he use to work before he got wit' Kyope.

When Crane nodded that he wanted the usual, *E & J Brandy* on ice, O seductively walked over to the table. I sat up straight to get a better view wit'out starin' too hard. And when I did, I saw Crane lookin' at me. We made eye contact a few times in the past and I never understood why. He always seemed to be focused on me. Like he was studyin' me or somethin'. Sometimes I thought he was on to me. And other times I charged it to bein' 'noid.

Anyway, O walked out like a superstar. Her body was unreal. I neva saw a waist so small that led to an ass so phat. She reminded me of my ex-girl Keisha and that jive fucked me up. She was obviously more loose than usual. She must've added a drink wit' her smoke. *Shiiiiittttt…*whateva she needed to do to make it work, I was wit'. And she had her victims captivated. Everyone but Spikes.

"Damn girl," Prangsta yelled damn near spillin' his drink on the table. "It's like that?" he continued admirin' her thick legs. I don't know but for some reason…it seemed like he was tryin' too hard.

O ain't acknowledge shit they was sayin'. She moved a few drinks on the table they surrounded and eased on top of it. She held the red net purse that protected her possessions closely.

Sittin' on the table, she leaned back so that her legs could sway back and forth in the air like scissors. Movin' her thongs to the side, she winked at them as she showed them her juice box. Prangsta and Crane stood up to get a better view, while Kyope eyed her from where he sat. Spikes acted as if she wasn't even there. In less than two minutes, O was able to get them to bring they guards down. It was exactly what we wanted.

"Damn!" Prangsta said grabbin' his dick. "You fat as shit! I can fuck that pussy right?"

She ignored the question and said, "If you like that than watch this," she smiled.

Taking Kyope's empty Corona bottle, she injected it slowly into her pussy. Then she threw her head back and her golden colored hair fell on her shoulders before brushin' the table lightly. Niggas wit' camera phones was in full flick mode. O was killin' 'em and now she had the attention of other people in the area too. The girl on the stage dancin' sat down on the edge and watched. For this moment, she was gettin' no love. O performed like she was enjoyin' every minute of it and for a second, I wondered if she did.

"Mmmmmmm," she moaned, movin' her hips while they watched like young doctors witnessin' the birth of a baby. She was fuckin' the shit out that bottle. Archin' her back like it had hit her spot.

Kyope sat in his chair and peeled off a couple of hundreds and the others threw what they had left. Money appeared to fall from the sky as strippers looked on in envy. There had to be over three thousand dollars on the table and a couple hundred in the air.

"You, boys ready for me?" she asked Kyope and his crew. They eyes told her they was ready. She pulled the bottle out of her wetness and placed it on the table. Prangsta grabbed it and sucked the rim. A few niggas shook they heads in disgust. He stay goin' too far. Once she was up, she was careful 'bout keepin' her purse close to her at all times.

"Would you mind if I dance for you?" she asked Crane. He shook his head no. "You won't be disappointed," she winked.

Wit' her back faced Crane, she moved her hips around on his lap like the second hand on a clock. Havin' recently done me, I knew how good it felt. Crane grabbed a hold of her hips like handlebars on his first bike. She allowed him to. She took her time and didn't rush the show. Next she turned around to face him, and straddled him. Her feet ain't touch the floor and she moved like a spinnin' top. Everything was goin' as planned.

When she was done wit' him, she eased over to Prangsta who acted like he just got out of Cell Block 8. He snatched her by the arm and pulled her on top of him. For some reason, I felt like breakin' his jaw. I fell back realizin' that me smashin' his ass wasn't in the plan. Once again he was loud and boisterous puttin' on a show. I was startin' to wonder 'bout him.

"Damn! You make me wanna put somethin' in you right here and now," he said as she straddled him and placed her arms 'round his back.

"Be easy big, boy," she told him. "I just wanna make you feel good."

Wit' out anyone noticin', she looked at me like, *if this disgustin' mothafucka tries to fuck me I'ma cut his ass.* I quickly nodded to let her know she was doin' the damn thing and that I wouldn't let him go too far.

When the song was done, she hopped off him wit' the quickness and collected her money from the table and floor. The crowd dispersed. Some went on 'bout they business, while others looked for the stripper that could give O a run for her money. Smilin' one last time at me, O walked away. I knew it was done.

"Yo…that was the baddest bitch I ever laid eyes on!" Prangsta proclaimed.

"No doubt," Kyope co-signed. "I might have to put that young thing to work. She definitely looks like a keeper."

Crane unable to talk just smiled like a helpless child. O successfully played her position and now I was up. I got outta my seat, and eased over to they section. All of 'em stood when they saw me approach *except* Kyope. You woulda thought they was protectin' Jay-Z.

"Easy, fellas," I said holdin' out my hands. "I just wanna talk to Da Boss."

"Nigga, you betta step da fuck off," Prangsta said reachin' into his coat. I saw his face go from cockiness to fright when what he was lookin' for, wasn't there. A light smile came across mine. I directed my attention to Kyope.

"Like I said I'm here to see Da Boss. I'll step after that."

For a second I looked at him wonderin' if he recognized me despite my smoke colored shades concealing my eyes.

"Nigga, you betta get the fuck outta here," Spikes threatened. "I ain't gonna ask you again."

I knew Spikes wasn't strapped cuz he wasn't muscle. He was cocky on the strength of Crane and Prangsta. But the look in Crane's eyes told me that she'd also got him for his piece too.

She did her job well.

"Young, nigga...I advise you to talk quick. Cuz you bringin' down my high, and I don't like my high brought down," Kyope interrupted. Prangsta, Spikes and Crane mean mugged me as I spoke my piece.

"I wanna get put on." Kyope looked at me and then at his crew. They all laughed hysterically.

"Lil nigga, are you serious? Who the fuck are you?" Kyope continued.

"I'm from down south and I'm trynna get put on. I heard you can help me wit' that. I wanna work for you." Silence. Only the club music could be heard.

"Give me one reason why I should put you on?"

"For one, I can drop this nigga right where he stand," I said talkin' 'bout Prangsta. They all laughed again. My face was void of emotion.

When Kyope's laughs diminished he said, "Prove it."

"This nigga couldn't-,"

I don't know what Prangsta was 'bout to say but I laid him on his back. His body fell onto the table behind him. Bottles and cups toppled on his face and chest as he hit the floor. When he got his self up, he tried to step to me but Kyope stopped him.

"I ain't 'bout to just let this nigga hit me," Prangsta said as he rubbed his jaw.

"I already did, slim" I informed him.

Kyope's squad reached for their weapons, but again, nothing was there. I pulled out mine and aimed.

Kyope looked at Crane, Spikes and Prangsta. He must've been wonderin' where they heat was. Kyope was visibly disgusted. Prangsta continued to pat himself as if his gun would miraculously reappear. When Kyope looked toward the ceilin', and looked back down shakin' his head, I could tell it finally registered that O got them for they swammies.

"You got it, lil man," Kyope smiled obviously tight at his

squad. They acted like pitbulls ready to rip my throat out. The only thing stoppin' them was Kyope. "Everybody ease up. We all good here." Spectators stopped what they was doin' and waited for the next move. "Now...I'ma need you to put that piece up, before somebody get hurt." I looked at his squad makin' it clear wit'out words that I would use it if I had too. And then I tucked it in the back of my shirt. When it was put away, Kyope asked, "Why you wanna get put on?"

"Cuz I'm hungry. I'm up here by myself and not livin' the way I know I can. And judgin' by the looks of things, you need somebody you can count on." That verbal blow was for his crew. They grunted but I knew Kyope was wit me considerin' they let a bitch get 'em for they guns.

I was so impressed that I made them look like idiots that I ain't see Crane step away from Kyope and his crew. I guess he ain't *hear* when Kyope told them to fall back bein' as though he was deaf. Before I knew it, I was on the ground. Blood escaped my cracked lip. I could've gone two different ways. Got up, cracked him in his head to return the favor, or...let that shit ride seein' the bigger picture. For now, I let him have that.

"Just like I thought," I said touchin' my lip. "You need me cuz this nigga can't hit for shit."

Kyope prevented him from comin' at me again. If not...an all out war would've ensued.

"You gotta a lot of heart, young blood," he said sizin' me up. "Ain't no doubt you got balls. But you come in here, disrespect my crew and then hit my man in the face. Give me one reason why I should let you live? And before you answer, take your shades off."

Hesitantly I complied and said, "For starters, you need someone to have your back at all times. Just cuz pussy present don't mean you clock out. Your squad obviously forgot that."

"Why he even still talkin' Kyope?" Prangsta asked.

"Wait a minute," Kyope said like he remembered some-

thin'. He looked into my eyes. "Have we met?" The thumpin' of my heart moved my chest.

"Naw, slim."

"You sure?" He persisted. "I feel like I met you somewhere before."

"Never. I just be in this muthafucka day in and out. Now look, either you feelin' me or you not! I'm not 'bout to waste my time. What's it gonna be?"

There was a long period of silence before he said, "Let's talk." I got him! I placed my shades back on. "Meet me here next week so we can talk alone."

"You got it," I told him eager to get into this nigga's life and fuck shit up.

"But I got somethin' for you to do first."

"Name it."

"I need you to get my tools back and merk that bitch who took 'em. Tonight."

SATURDAY, 10:22 PM

****

Shit is finally movin' according to plan. Then why do I feel so fucked up?

-Kelsi

I had some time to kill before O met me at this pizza joint in the city. The small restaurant was overcrowded wit' New Yorkers gettin' slices wit' extra cheese. I sat quietly in the corner waitin' to see O, checkin' my surroundings in between. It had been five days since Kyope signed me on and I'd already started to wreak havoc. Kyope played me close though. He ain't tell me much. And wit' his crew peepin' errything I did and said…it was virtually impossible to do all the things I wanted done. Most of the shit I learned 'bout his operation I learned from askin' 'round 'bout "The Crown". I wanted to know which hoods was pumpin' it and who was in charge. Most of my research ended in vain. People thought I was a cop. But wit' the little info I did discover,

I was able to put a dent in his force that I was sure would sting Kyope's ass.

Last Night

"I gotta roll, man," Marble told his soldiers as he exited one of the buildings at the Nicholas Houses projects, in New York. It was a dark cool night and his two soldiers were manning the front. "I'ma be late."

"No problem, my dude," one of the two responded. "We got you. Just make sure you hit me off if you win big."

"If I win, I got you… no problemo," he lied. His Spanish accent was thick as normal. "Just make sure you hold shit down out here. We still don't know who this fool is shuttin' down our shit. Kyope wants us to keep our eyes peeled."

"No doubt. You just watch your own ass."

"Please," he said waving them off. "Ain't nobody crazy 'nough to fuck wit' me." With that he dipped off. Kyope's men had a tendency to think they were untouchable.

All he was thinking about was rushing to his truck which held his white prize winning pit bull, Ether, in the back seat. His mind was on taking him to a match to see him rip another dog's throat out. Ether won every match he entered. On a tight schedule, Marble jogged to his old navy blue Suburban. He had twenty minutes to make it to his destination. Time was of the essence.

Standing about five feet tall, they called him Marble because although he claimed not to have any African American in him, everyone was pretty sure he did. His hair was a little kinkier than other people of Spanish descent.

"Aight, Ether!" he said opening his car door and sliding inside. "You gotta win big tonight, papi! I'm tryin' to cop that new Beamer. "Noticing the dog was silent he turned around and saw him lying comfortably on the back seat.

"Ether," he said as he drove down W 127th slowly. "I know you ain't sleep. We got too much to…-,"

Before he could get out another word, from the third row

seat, Kelsi sent a bullet through his head which exited out the front window. Marble didn't know what hit him. The truck rolled into a few cars parked along the street and stopped. Earlier Kelsi had placed crushed up Tylenol PM in some fresh ground beef and thrown it inside the window Marble left down to give the dog some air. He waited patiently for the dog to drift off to sleep and entered waiting for Marble. With Marble executed, he exited.

"Stupid ass, nigga," Kelsi said out loud. "Got caught slippin'."

Slumpin' Marble was definitely a good look cuz he had been wit' Kyope forever. Marble had killed so many in the name of business, that niggas was afraid to fuck wit' his operation. But I wasn't the average nigga. I was a nigga on a mission. While waitin' on O, I decided to call my lil brother, Lorenzo Jr. Before I left Maryland, I could tell he was fucked up that I was leavin'. I spent a lot of time wit' him before I left. Wit' my mother dead, he was the only person alive I considered family. The doctors called him retarded but I knew he understood more than people gave him credit for.

Thinkin' 'bout the reason he was retarded was fucked up. Our so-called father beat his mother while she was pregnant tryin' to make her miscarry. It seems being a father wasn't the only thing he ain't do right, cuz my brother survived. Sometimes I wish me and my moms had gone through wit' murderin' my father for the insurance money. Either way I'm sure he'll rot in hell sooner or later.

"Where you at big, brother? And how come you don't live here no more?" I looked around the restaurant focusin' on random people. Random faces.

"I'll be there when I can," I told him. Truth was…I ain't know if I was ever goin' back to Shelly's. One things for sure, I wasn't thinkin' 'bout leavin' New York 'til I dealt wit' Jarvis and Kyope.

"You wit' your mommy?" he asked soundin' like a two year old kid, even though we the same age.

"Naw, man...I wish I was."

I wasn't 'bout to waste time explainin' to him that my mother was murdered and that I missed her everyday of my life. I breathed out heavily and played wit' the white napkin on the table, lookin' up once more to see if O was on her way in. She wasn't.

And then I heard, "Who you talking to J.R?!"

It was Shelly. I sat up straight preparin' myself to talk to this bitch. She may have been his moms but she wasn't mine and I was tired of her questionin' me like I was a kid. Before the boy could answer she'd snatched the phone out his hands.

"Kelsi, is that you?" her voice irritated yet concerned.

"Yeah."

"Kelsi, where are you? Do you realize how worried me and your father have been? And that Nick Fearson person has been by here a lot. He said he tryin' to solve your mother's murder and Delonte's."

That cop was gettin' on my nerve! Delonte was dead and my mother was gone! Fuck he want with me?

"Listen...I told you I got some shit to handle. When I'm done I'll be back. And tell that cop he can suck my dick."

"Watch your tone!"

"Whateva, Shelly."

"You betta not be gettin' in no trouble, Kelsi. You still a child." She was wrong.

I wasn't. I seen and did too much dirt to ever be able to call myself a kid. "Cuz if you get in trouble, it'll be your own fault," she continued. "And just so you know I filed a missing person's report on you."

"Whateva, Shelly," She was five seconds from gettin'

cussed the fuck out. "I just called to check on J.R. don't worry 'bout me, I'm good."

Without waitin' for a response I hung up. And the moment I did, O slow rolled past the front of the restaurant in a red Altima with New York City license plates looking for a place to park. When she walked in, she was wearin' a tight pink velour sweat suit. Her hair was pulled back into a tight ponytail and I couldn't help but smile at her natural beauty. She eased into the booth style seat directly in front of me.

"What's goin' on, Aven?" she asked, her nose was beet red. "Why you wanna meet me so late?" I ain't been 'round her a lot, but from what I could tell, when she was nervous, her nose turned red.

"You nervous?"

"No. She lied. I just wanna know why I'm here."

"It's only 10:00, O."

"It's after 10:00," she said as she placed her purse on the table, rubbed her hair wit' her hand and waited. "Plus you know I gotta dance tonight."

"You hungry?"

"No," she said foldin' her hands in front of her.

"Okay," I said as I looked down at the worn white table. What was wrong wit' me? Why was I findin' it so hard to be real wit' her? "Bout that spot...you don't dance there no more."

"What?"

"You can't work there no more." I repeated.

"I wasn't gonna leave until *next* month," she advised thinkin' I was talkin' 'bout her movin' back to Atlanta. "I wanna save up some more money first."

"O...You don't work there no more startin' tonight. I'm not fuckin' playin'. It's ova for you there."

"Explain, Aven."

"Them niggas you got for they guns ordered me to kill you. So unless you wanna die...you don't work there no more."

"But...," her voice trailed.

"You wanna die?"

"No...but...why kill *me*?" she asked pointin' at herself. She looked confused. Like she couldn't find the logic.

"Yes. Kill you," I pointed back at her. "And you have to move, too."

"But why?" she persisted.

"It's all a game to them, O. They don't give a fuck 'bout you, my moms, or nobody else!"

"Your moms?"

I made a mistake and was angry at myself.

"I mean...they don't give a fuck 'bout nobody. Trust me, I know."

"Aven...this is too quick, where am I gonna go?" she asked lookin' 'round the crowded restaurant. I think she was worried somebody was gonna walk up and shoot her right there.

"Nobody's gonna hurt you while I'm here, O. You good. Relax." She dropped her head and shook it.

I felt fucked up for puttin' her in this predicament, but I needed her to do what I wanted done. My part of the plan worked. I was in. A part of me started to believe she was ungrateful. She should be happy I wasn't gonna smoke her and be done wit' it. The worse part of me was willin' to do whatever it took to get closer to them, even if it did mean killin' her.

"Okay...I don't work there no more," she must've detected that I was growin' frustrated. "I'll find another place in New York somewhere before I go back to Atlanta."

"That's not good enough. You gotta move outta state."

"What?!" she yelled causin' people to stare. "Why outta state?"

"Stop actin' like you don't know what the deal is. And lower your fuckin' voice," I demanded through clenched teeth. I wasn't up for the show.

"But over some guns?"

"Naw…ova the principle. They feel played and they wanna see how far I'll go to get wit' 'em."

"How bad *do* you want to be with 'em?" she asked nervously.

"I'd give my life to get closer to Kyope." I confirmed. "But you safe. If I wanted to hurt you, you'd be dead by now."

"Why is this so important to you? Why is gettin' with him so important?"

"You askin' the questions you don't really want the answers to."

"But this doesn't make any sense, Aven," she said switchin' the subject. "I can't leave right now. Where am I gonna go?"

"On a plane! What's so fuckin' hard to understand?"

"But…I ain't got no place to go really in Atlanta either. Most of my people can barely take care of themselves right now. I wasn't supposed to go back needing help. I was supposed to go back different. Successful," she looked up at me wit' sad eyes.

When she started cryin', I wanted to wrap my arms around her. But an unseen wall kept me in my place and her vulnerability was startin' to make me irritated. Suddenly I became angry. Why was she whinin'? And why did I always find myself involved in some emotional bullshit? I'm sick of this shit. All I care 'bout is revenge.

"Look," I said as I stood up. "I'm sorry shit got fucked up for you, but this right here…ain't for me."

I reached in my pocket and dropped four thousand dollars on the table. One of the dirty bills brushed her face as if found its way down. I'm sure she had dirty money thrown at her before. And it was two thousand more than she thought she was gettin'.

"Aven…are you leaving me alone?"

"I'm not your man, O."

"But…but you said you wouldn't let anything happen to me," she cried standin' wit'out collectin' the money.

"Sorry, O. I'm out," I moved quickly to the door.

"Please, Aven. Don't leave me. I'm beggin' you."

I paused before walkin' out the glass door. People stared at us. I felt heavy turnin' my back on her but what was I 'sposed to do? Fuckin' wit' O would cause more problems than I was tryin' to deal wit'.

"Take care, shawty," I told her pushin' forward. When I went outside and flagged a cab, the look on her face stayed wit' me. Her tears. Her pleas. Everything she said 'bout me not leavin' her and protectin' her played in my mind like a movie.

"Fuck!" I said out loud. A white woman walkin' by jumped nervously. I was surprised when a cabby stopped.

"Where to?" he asked after I jumped in.

I told him.

Feelin' guilty, and wit'out thinkin', I punched the back of his seat. He looked at me through his rearview mirror.

"What the fuck my, friend!!! Everythin' alright?" the cab driver asked wit' a Pakistan accent.

I ignored him. What did he think?

Instead of responding, I stared at the large billboards in the city and tried to focus on my next move. Fuck I care 'bout a bitch I just met? I'm a soldier. And soldiers don't need nothin' or nobody holdin' them back. So why was I sayin', "Turn around."

"What?"

"I said turn around. I forgot somethin' at the restaurant."

"You people are somethin' else," he said under his breath.

The moment he whipped the car around, I reached through the small window separatin' us and punched him in the back of his head. The cab came to a complete stop.

"Get out!!!!" he screamed holdin' the back of his head. I angrily jumped out.

What was goin' on wit' me? Why was I lettin' this broad get under my skin?

I walked back to the restaurant my hand throbbin' from

lashin' out. But when I reached the spot, I ain't see O through the large window. Had she gone? I walked in and looked for her. For some reason...I felt fucked up. I shook my head and breathed out cuz I knew she was just like me. Out here alone, and on a mission. For some reason my mother came to mind. I wondered what she must've gone through when she was in New York alone. Maybe if she had someone to care for her, she would've had an easier life. But who was I? *Captain Save A Ho?*

I turned 'round to leave 'til I heard, "Aven?" I stopped, turned back around and faced her. She had just stepped out of the bathroom. A smile came across her face. "I thought you left me." Silence. I walked up to her...she met me halfway.

"Look...you can stay wit' me for a few days. I got a crib over on 29th and Crescent in Queens. I'm movin' in tomorrow."

It was a one bedroom joint I found a few weeks back. It was small but plenty for me. The landlord ain't ask questions and gladly accepted the six months rent in advance I'd given him.

"Thank you, Aven," she said softly wrappin' her arms 'round my neck. "Thank you for not leavin' me." I found myself smilin' inside.

"Listen," I said pushin' her away. "I'm lettin' you stay wit' me cuz all this kinda my fault. But there are some rules you gotta understand before we do any of this shit."

"I'm listenin', Aven," she said softly. "Anything you want."

"I can't have you askin' a bunch of questions about what I do when I leave my crib. And most of all, don't tell *NOBODY* you stayin' wit' me. 'Specially none of them cacklin' bitches at Waves."

"Okay."

"I'm serious, shawty," I pointed at her.

"Okaaaay, Aven. Whateva you want. I understand."

"Seriously, don't ever ask me 'bout my life. If I don't tell you it's cuz I don't want you to know. We ain't together and this arrangement is only til' shit blow over. Got it?"

"Yes, Aven," she giggled. "Nobody will know anything and I understand I'm not your girl. For now." I cut her a serious look. "Just playin'. I'm just so happy you didn't leave me."

She was shakin' her head and agreein' wit' me but a part of me wanted to say, *'fuck this shit it ain't gonna work'.* I knew bitches thought they could change a nigga but again, I ain't no ordinary nigga.

"Let's get outta here," I told her. "Where you park?"

"Round the corner, Aven," she said softly. I could tell from the smile on her face that she ain't understand what was really goin' on, but I let her have her moment. After all, she helped me get closer to mine.

The good thing about it is, she ain't know my real name and I ain't know hers. And as far as I was concerned, it could stay that way. The less we knew 'bout each other the better. Cuz I was certain our arrangement wouldn't last.

SATURDAY, 11:32 PM

****

Since I was a kid I never had a place to call home. Why should now be any different?

-O.

"I gotta leave, Jelly. They wanna kill me," O said as she drove to her apartment to gather her things. She had just dropped Kelsi off in Queens and he told her to only take what she could carry by hand. They separated because he didn't want to be seen with her in case Kyope was watching him.

"Why you gotta leave ova that dumb shit?" O had already briefed her on what Kelsi had her do to Kyope a few days back at the club. O was too naïve to understand the importance of being quiet despite Kelsi's warning.

"Cuz they trippin' that's why."

"Well where you gonna stay? You welcome to stay at my crib. It's small but I got room." O was thankful she at least offered. Because before Kelsi came back to the restaurant, she didn't think anybody else cared.

"Naw, I can't do that," she said softly. "I'm stayin' wit' Aven and he don't want me tellin' nobody. He'd be pissed if he found out I told you. But I had to tell you in case something happened to me."

"So you stayin' wit' the same nigga who got you caught up in all this shit? Is that smart, O?" She didn't respond. "He seems weird," Jelly continued.

The only reason she said he was weird to Jelly was because he never gave any of the other strippers the time of day, including her. Jelly had done everything from offering to give him a free lap dance, to test driving her worn out pussy. No matter what he refused.

"He's not weird, just cautious."

"So what...he don't want you to have no friends?"

"It's not even like that. We not together."

"You sure?"

"Yes. He's just tryin' to protect me," she said as she pulled up a few blocks from her apartment in Brooklyn. She avoided pulling directly in front in case someone was waiting to hurt her. The streets were dark and she couldn't see clearly.

"Humph...you betta be careful. He sounds like a controllin' ass nigga to me," Jelly complained. "But let me go, girl. I gotta make this money. Some ballas just came in here and they spendin' plenty cash."

O giggled and said, "Get that money! Later!"

While O thought about her situation, a light smile spread across her face. The best thing about leaving was that she wouldn't have to dance anymore. O had dreams of owning her own nightclub. But first, she'd have to wait for things to die down. She hoped she could count on Aven to protect her. In fact she prayed on it.

WEDNESDAY, 12:42 AM

****

Bein' the Boss ain't a luxury, it's a liability.

-Kyope

Kyope agreed to meet D-9 at an undisclosed location. So there would be no mistakes, Kyope had D-9 picked up. And when they arrived at the destination, they were in front of an old apartment building in Queens, New York. D-9 decided to meet with him because as Jarvis promised, he'd beat his grandmother repeatedly. And as it stood, she was on her death bed. Kyope didn't agree with Jarvis's tactics on finding out who was robbing their stash houses, but his unconventional plan worked.

When D-9 exited the car, he was directed to the building's entrance. Once inside, he was instructed to walk down a dark stairwell.

"Go straight downstairs," said the driver pointing. "Kyope will be inside."

"O…okay," he said nervously taking one last look at the

driver. He felt a strange sense of comfort with him considering he arrived in one peace.

The stairwell led to a cold basement. Inside, Kyope stood in front of three men. He recognized Prangsta and Crane but not the third man. D-9's albino colored skin finally got its color due to his blood rushing to the surface. He was terrified.

Kyope called Jarvis to tell him that he finally found D-9 but he wasn't answering his calls. Kyope wanted Jarvis to deal with this matter since it was his shops that had been hit lately. But lately Jarvis hadn't been the same. And he wondered if Steele's death had anything to do with it.

"Have a seat," Kyope said calmly. It was the only chair in the room. Kyope's kind jester put D-9 at slight ease.

Pwwwww. Bwwwwww. A foul odor escaped his body.

"Relax. Everything gonna be okay," Kyope said, fanning the air. D-9 took his seat looking at Prangsta, Crane and Kelsi who remained like soldiers standing in a line up.

"I'm glad you finally came out," Kyope started. "I hated how things have been for your grandmother. Shit's real fucked up ain't it?"

"I know, man. I ain't do nothin' though," D-9 shivered. "I know what Jarvis think, but it ain't me. I ain't been robbin' your houses. I would neva do nothin' like that man. Ya'll been too good to me."

"So why you runnin'?" Prangsta asked.

"I was scared cuz I knew what people was sayin'."

"Easy…easy," Kyope said in a soothing tone. "Aye Prangsta, go get him one of them beers in the fridge."

"No problem, Boss," Prangsta said stepping out of the line up.

When he returned, he handed D-9 the beer. His hand shook so badly, he almost dropped it, so he sat it down on the gray concrete floor beside him. Kyope walked up, and knelt down in front of him.

In an easy voice he said, "We just want you to tell us, what you know 'bout the recent robberies. That's it, man, and then, you free to go your way."

"I'm tellin' you, Kyope, I don't know shit," he said again. "If I knew who was fuckin' wit' your operation, I would've told you. I don't know what happened to Marble eitha. I'm loyal to you, Kyope! I swear on my grandmother's life. That's why I'm here man. I coulda ran like a bitch but I'm here." Kyope stood up and looked down at him.

"So you don't know nothin' 'bout who's been hittin' my shops or who killed Marble?"

"Nothin'," D-9 whined looking up at him. "I swear to God, Kyope! I promise I ain't got nothin' to do wit' this shit here." Kyope looked back at his crew and then at D-9.

"Well, I guess you free to be with you grandmother."

"For real, Kyope?" he asked hopefully. "This is finally over for real?"

"Yeah…it's done."

With that he walked back toward Kelsi and whispered something in his ear. And then Kelsi stepped up, drew his desert eagle and unloaded multiple bullets in his face. D-9's blood splattered on his clothes and he wiped it with the back of his hand. Kelsi hated putting in work for a man he was trying to bring down, but all this was needed to make things crumble.

"Good work," Kyope said placing his hand on Kelsi's shoulder. "Get rid of the body," he told Prangsta and Crane. Kelsi's skin crawled when he felt his touch but he didn't move.

"I don't think he was lyin'," Kelsi said so that only Kyope could hear him. He watched Crane and Prangsta lift D-9's lifeless body. "I been hearin' that Jarvis ain't been managin' shops no more. I know I ain't meet 'em yet, but it don't look good."

"I know he wasn't lyin'," Kyope confirmed. "But a statement had to be made, and it had to be made wit' him. He shouldn'tve ran. Maybe whoever is fuckin' wit' my money and my crew will think twice now."

Kyope wiped his hands with the handkerchief he kept in his pants pocket. And gave the dirty cloth to Kelsi to wipe his face.

Kelsi didn't use it.

"Anyway, he wanted to be wit' his grandmother, and I gave the order to kill her over an hour ago. They together now."

Kelsi looked at him like he wanted to rip his heart out. It was one thing to murder a street dude in the game but where was the honor in killing an old woman?

"You aight?" Kyope asked picking up on the evil glare in Kelsi's eyes. Kelsi realizing his error straightened up his face.

"Yeah...I'm cool. Just don't know why you got Jarvis 'round you if you know he fuckin' up."

Kyope smiled. After only a short time, he already liked him. He felt he had heart. Kyope ordered Kelsi to kill three people and he murdered each one of them without flinching. Although Kyope was in his early forties, he felt he was getting too old for the game. He was looking for someone he could trust to take over. Originally he thought it would be Jarvis. But he was just as old as him and not as wise. He felt Kelsi had a warrior spirit and he needed someone like him around.

"Aight, let's roll," Kyope told him. "I know a place that makes a hell of a fried steak."

Kelsi went but he wouldn't forget.

THURSDAY, 12:42 PM

****

Ever since I could remember I loved to floss.

-Kenosha

TWO MONTHS LATER

People rushed up and down the block as I hustled toward Jarvis's car. He'd given me some money to go shopping while he handled business. Ever since I'd been with him, life had been good. And just like most men after a few months of knowing me, he started spoiling me rotten. I made a decision that there was no reason for me to continue to lie to Skully about following Kelsi. I was going to come clean with him today. Not to mention I ain't even know where Kelsi was or what he was doing.

"Doby, I'll be right back," I told the driver after we pulled up to the cheap motel room I maintained. I had access to the May Bach whenever I wanted.

When I looked out the window and at the motel I sighed. I didn't want to go in or near this funky ass spot. The only reason I kept it was for Skully. If he followed me, I wanted him to think I was still here.

"Not a problem, ma'am," he smiled opening the car door for me. "I'll be right here when you get back." I had just gotten off of the phone with Jarvis and he asked me to stay with him for a while. I know it's crazy, but we'd done so much together, it brought us closer.

Once inside the room, I gathered most of my things and sat them on the bed. I realized I had to pee before I left and went to the bathroom. I squatted and let the warm liquid escape my vagina when I heard the front door open.

"Who's that?" I screamed from the toilet. *Silence.* "Doby...is that you?" *Silence.* I grabbed a piece of tissue, lifted up a little, and wiped myself. And before I could get my panties on, the door opened. A figure walked in and closed the door behind them.

"There you go," he said in a low tone. I didn't recognize the voice.

"Who the fuck are you?!" I yelled trying to reach for the light switch

He grabbed me and covered my mouth with his rough hand. Then he grabbed my hair with his other hand and pulled me down to the floor. I fought but was no match for his strength. After flinging me around, he stood me back up causing me to be off balance. With my back faced him, he shoved his fingers roughly inside of me.

"That pussy still wet," he said in my ear. "If you're good and quiet, I'll let you piss on me, baby." His voice was husky and gross. He pressed his hands tightly against my lips and I could feel the sweat from his upper lip against my face. "I want you to suck my dick real quick," he continued. "It won't take me long to cum in that pretty mouth of yours. I'll let you swallow every drop too. So what do you say, honey? You wanna swallow?"

"P...please, stop," I mumbled through his fingers.

My quick movements allowed his rough fingers to slide deeper into me. I was scared. "Now I'ma let you go," he said. "And then you gonna suck my dick, aight? But you gotta do it quick. Or we gonna get caught."

He was just about to make me suck his dick when the door opened and the light in the bathroom came on.

"What the fuck you doin'?"

I knew that voice well and the face belonged to Skully.

"Uh…nothin'," he said still holding my mouth, his fingers still inside me. "I thought she was goin' scream so I covered her mouth."

"Is that's why your finger inside of her?" He didn't respond. "Just bring her out here," he said without caring that he was violating me. Skully disappeared into the bedroom area.

"You lucky," he told me, my pussy still sore as he sucked his fingers. "Real lucky."

Without time to prepare for his next move, he pulled me into the bedroom by my hair. Skully's platinum skull necklace with the diamonds in it stood out when we made it to the bedroom. The medallion was definitely bigger than the one he use to wear. Now in the light of the room, I could see who the rapist was. He was white and obese and I'd seen him with Skully before.

"Look at this, bitch!" Skully laughed as I was hoisted on the top of the bed by his goon. Skully's skin was still ashy black and his eyes were still bloodshot red. He walked up to me and slapped me in the face. As if I was his enemy, he hit me repeatedly all over my body.

"Skully, please stop! You hurting me." Wrapping his fingers around a wad of my hair, he pulled it tightly.

"Going somewhere?" he asked pointing at the bags.

He pushed my bags on the floor. It was then that I noticed along with the white man, there was another dark short man there. Both were wearing jeans and coats and their expressions were motionless. The white man smirked taking another glimpse of my pussy.

"What the fuck is up, Kenosha?" Skully asked.

Before answering him, I covered my partially naked body from the waist down with the sheet on the bed. And he grabbed the sheet off and jammed two of his fingers inside of me.

"Plllllllllllleasssssssssssssssssssse stop, Skully!" I lifted my head and cursed the ceiling I was in so much pain. "Why you hurting me?"

"Shut up you dumb, bitch! You thought you was gonna just take my money and get away wit' it? Huh? You had a job to do, Kenosha. You forgot about it that quick?!"

When he was done amusing the men who were laughing, he pushed the two fingers that were inside of me in my mouth.

"You think your pussy tastes good enough for me to let you live even though you been dodgin' me?" I silently wept. "Do you!" he screamed. "One of ya'll wanna taste this shit to see if it's worth the thousands of dollars I spent on it?" he asked them.

My heart dropped. Here he was treating me like he didn't know me. I felt like a freak. I felt like less than a person. I would've called out to God for his help but I've done so much shit I know he wouldn't recognize me.

The white man quickly took Skully up on his offer. He slid on the bed, placed his hands on each of my knees and licked my pussy. His tongue was rough and felt nasty.

"Yeah...she tastes real good, man." He said getting up licking all of my juices from his mouth with his tongue. "It's not thousands of dollars worth though."

Tears drained my eyes and it disgusted me when he got up because I could see the hardness of his dick.

"Don't worry, Jax," Skully started. "I'ma let you fuck this bitch when I'm done wit' her. But let me handle my business first." The man walked back over against the wall and winked at me squeezing his hard dick through his jeans.

"Now…what have you been doing, Kenosha?"

"I'm tryin'."

"You tryin'?" he laughed. "Obviously not hard enough. You haven't been answerin' my calls *yet* you been spendin' my money," he said looking at the clothes on the floor. I was not about to tell him his money was gone along time ago and that I was now spending his arch enemy's cash. "So what's up? And how come that mothafuckin' nigga Jarvis still breathin'? I thought you was gonna make sure Kelsi took care of things two months ago?"

"I've been trying, Skully," I cried as the rippling sensation in my scalp took over. "But Kelsi says he got somethin' else planned."

"Like what, Kenosha?"

"I don't know. He wouldn't tell me."

"So let me get this straight, you out here on my dolla and you don't know shit and ain't been doin' shit?"

"Skully, please…just give me some more time. I swear I'll get Kelsi to do him."

As I looked at his face, I was surprised that such a dark skinned man could turn red. A vein had presented itself on the middle of his forehead and I could see it pulsating. As always his eyes were red and my heart began to beat faster. What was next?

Skully never treated me like this in all the time I've known him. I was always his main girl and he never hurt me. I wasn't sure but I had a feeling his anger had more to do with jealousy than it did with Jarvis still being alive.

"You wouldn't be tryin' to fuck me over now would you, Kenosha?" he asked me as he straddled my body, looking down at me. I shook my head no. "Cuz you know what I'd do to you right?" I nodded yes. "What will I do to you, Kenosha?" his voice steady, deep and cold.

"Make me wish I was neva born." I whimpered.

"Exactly," he smiled. "Jax!"

"Yes, sir!" he said excitedly.

"You can fuck this bitch," he said looking at me. "I'll be waiting on you out in the car."

Monday, 10:58 pm

****

Niggas gotta understand that business and females can't co-exist. And most niggas can't do it.

-Kyope

Kyope was in his penthouse fucking his main girl. Her toes curled as he pressed further into her back, gripping her ass for control.

"Ahhhhhhhh….," she moaned. "I love you, papi." Her white skin was flushed and her golden hair dressed the bed. If a picture was taken of their lovemaking, it would come out flawless. Pressing his tongue into her mouth, he felt himself preparing to let go inside of her. Kristal Kerry had a way of squeezing the walls of her pussy bringing the hardest of niggas to their knees.

"Keep it right there, bitch," he demanded. "Just like that."

"Whateva you want, papi. I'm not goin' nowhere."

He was feeling her sex on all levels. And then his red phone rang. The only time it rang was in extreme emergencies. No longer excited about busting a nut, he pulled out of her seconds before being able to release.

"What's up?" he said grabbing the receiver. Kristal sat up and grabbed the covers to hide her lonely body. She hated how she always had to play the backseat when it came to his operation.

"Yo, Kyope...you seen Jarvis?!" Spikes yelled into the receiver. "A lot of fucked up shit just happened!"

"Like what?" he asked sitting up straight in the bed.

"Well anotha one of his shops got taken down tonight and we can't find him."

"Which one?"

"The main one, in Brooklyn." The room appeared to be spinning. Although sitting down, Kyope felt off balance. "They took everything, boss. We just dropped off the re-up before it happened. We lost five men too!"

Kyope was furious and said, "How'd it happen?"

"I'm not sure. Niggas sayin' some broads did it and others sayin' some dudes ran in. Whoever it was got in and out in ten minutes flat."

ONE WEEK EARLIER

Kelsi sat on the weight bench in his jeans and white wife beater inside his hotel room. He was making progress with breaking down Kyope's empire one captain at a time, but it wasn't enough to cause the havoc he wanted. He wanted worlds rocked and lifestyles stopped. And then he learned that one of the main shops was located in Brooklyn. But with the man power Kyope possessed, he wouldn't be able to infiltrate alone. With the phone in hand, he dialed his old friend's number. He had it saved to memory.

The phone rang twice before he answered, "Who this?" Silence. "Who the fuck is this?"

"It's me, man." Kelsi said reluctantly. He contemplated hanging up. Maybe it was a bad idea.

Silence.

"Kelsi?"

"Yeah, Bricks. It's me. I need your help."

Bricks hadn't heard from Kelsi since Kelsi accused him of fucking his ex-girlfriend Keisha before he himself killed her. Kelsi feared he'd reject him, after all, he'd let a female come between their bond.

"Fuck you waitin' on, nigga! You gonna give me the address or what? I'll be on my way."

Kelsi   smiled,   and   the   rest   was   history.

EARLIER TONIGHT

Bricks arranged for twenty niggas to come down from D.C., to help Kelsi take down Kyope and Jarvis' main shop. Every person with him was part of Brick's family, including his brother Melvin. Five of his crewmembers included his girl cousins. Every one of them was involved in the drug business and jumped at a chance to hit up some New York niggas for a big score.

Kelsi called it operation, Shock Factor. The plan was simple. They would travel in five vehicles. The first car would have the five girls and it would be followed by vans which would collect the product and money. Kelsi was surprised at how quickly Bricks got things together. He didn't realize that since he had left Maryland, Bricks had graduated from small time drug dealer to full fledge Goon status.

The streets were busy and it was hot outside of the large house in Brooklyn. And there were four men guarding the stash house they were interested in. The street soldiers had no clue what would happen next.

"Help! Help!" one of the five girls in a convertible silver Mercedes screamed. They pulled up in front of the house in distress. "My friend is in labor! Please!"

All four of the men grabbed their waists suspecting foul play until they saw her large stomach, and red fluid all over the white leather seats. The other four women looked like they were on their way to the club before things happened.

"Fuck is up wit' ya'll?" the tallest of the four said.

"My friend is pregnant and she 'bout to have this baby! Can you please tell us how to get to the hospital?!"

One of the men noticed their New Jersey tags and thought the stupid girls got lost and needed help finding their way back. Still, he wasn't feeling the scene. He scanned the car for a GPS system. Surely an expensive vehicle like this should have one. It didn't.

"I don't know what to tell you," he said while the other men remained silent. "I ain't got GPS on my face."

"Please! I ain't gonna make it!" the pregnant girl screamed. "Do somethin'! Shit!"

"Can you at least tell us how far the nearest hospital is?!" the driver screamed at the men. "I'll find it by myself since ya'll too weak to help!"

"Call the ambulance!" the pregnant girl hollered. "Call now!"

Not wanting extra attention around the house, since they had new product and it was the first of the month, they decided to point the broads in the right direction.

Walking up to the car, the tallest was about to give directions. His eyes widened when he saw the machine guns lying on the floor of the car. His head was blown into pieces before he could object or warn his friends. Blood and guts were all over the car with the stolen plates.

The other four men were about to unleash but were no match for the girls. The women stood up in the car, and lit the house up with heavy machinery, including the one who was really pregnant with the fake blood covered on her body. Now, she had the fresh blood of strangers on her. Exactly on schedule, the four vans pulled in front of the house and the men jumped out. They were also toting major weapons.

Hearing the commotion, a few of the soldiers inside the house knocked out windows and started shooting outside. But they were no match for the firepower Brick's crew possessed. The house was rushed by Brick's crew. In ten minutes flat, they managed to unload the house of the money and weight.

Two of the girls suffered bullet wounds but were okay. They looked at it as a small price to pay for fortune. After all, the crew escaped with over a million dollars worth of dope and five hundred thousand dollars worth of cash.

And Kelsi sat in the last van watching, smiling, and loving it all.

CURRENTLY

"What you want us to do?" Spikes asked waiting on Kyope's response. "It's the first so we gonna lose a lot of business."

"Fuck!" Kyope yelled exiting the bed, exposing his naked body and now limp dick.

"I'ma make a few calls. A few niggas owe me some favors. But we won't be back up and runnin' 'til next week. We have to play it easy cuz NYPD is gonna be everywhere now. We need to lay low. Have somebody burn that house."

"I know," Spikes added. "We already did. This shit really hurt us, man" he continued.

"I'ma need you to find Jarvis, tonight," Kyope griped.

"Bet."

"I'm not playin' games wit' him no more."

"I know he met some bitch awhile back. Prangsta said she be wit' him all the time. Said they just came back from Miami and shit too."

"Another bitch huh?"

Kyope was sick of Jarvis's need for a fairytale lifestyle. He was also tired of him not being able to handle business every time he got a new chick in his life. It was all or nothing with him and his carelessness has interfered with business greatly. His antics had caused their billion dollar status to drop to millions. Why couldn't he just get his dick wet and maintain his shops? He would've slumped Jarvis a long time ago but nobody provoked fear and commanded an army like Jarvis could.

"Yeah...he doin' it again," Spikes confirmed. "What you want me to do?"

Kyope walked up to his mirror, looked at himself and dropped his head.

Sighing heavily into the phone he said, "Find out where this bitch lay her head and send a message."

"A final one?" Spikes needed clarification.

"Leave a message he won't forget."

"Nuff said."

WEDNESDAY, 12:13 PM

****

*I wonder if my mother sees the gangsta I've become.
And respect's it.*

-Kelsi

She got a habit.

One I like.

Every Friday wit'out fail, she get on the New York City subway and take the train to Manhattan. She loves to shop. And I ain't goin' lie, Kyope keep this bitch laced. Designer fits and big ass diamonds. I ain't into white broads, but in a different life, she'd be one I'd definitely fuck. I wanted to make sure the time was right before I pushed off and added that bitch to my list of casualties. But after Bricks helped me knock down Kyope's main shop, I felt inspired and motivated to vanish her earlier than expected. I heard voices tellin' me to merk this bitch and merk her tonight. So…I decided to listen.

The train was full of New Yorkers doin' regular shit. But

me...I kept my eyes on the *white* woman in *white*. I followed her wit' each transfer she made and was careful to keep my distance. It seemed like no one was around but me and her. And the gun in my waist felt alive. Like it was talkin' to me. After awhile, I was growin' weary at not bein' able to step off from everybody else so I could send her ass on her way. And then...finally, she got off the train. I followed her up the escalator leadin' outside. She had an iphone and appeared captivated by its music.

It was perfect. The greater the diversion the better. The moment we stepped off the escalator, I carefully placed my blue hood on my head and walked up to her slowly. And then she turned around.

"Aven?" she said as if it were a question.

"Yeah...bi-," before I could reach under my jacket and blow her brains out, I saw Crane.

He stepped in front of her, and looked down at me. His 6'4 inch frame towered over mine. He was wearin' the same dingy blue uniform he always did. His presence was powerful and for some reason, I was humbled by it. Turns out he was wit' her the entire time. I just ain't see him 'til now. I was fuckin' up. I felt like I was goin' crazy. How could I overlook some major shit like that?

"Aven...everything okay?" she asked talkin' around Crane.

"Oh...uh...yeah. Everything cool. You know wit' all this stuff happenin', I just wanted to make sure you was good. You shouldn't be out here by yourself."

She giggled. "Thank you...but Crane follows me sometimes. Kyope swears I need protection every now and again, but for real I don't."

I looked up at Crane and he stared at me like he wanted to kill me. Like he was tryin' to figure me out. I looked away before he read my whole plan. I know this nigga hated me, and he had every right to.

"Well," I said takin' one last look up at him. "As long as he watchin' you, I'll roll."

"I'll talk to you later," I told her turnin' around.

"Bye, Aven."

She was talkin' to my back, I was already gone.

"Damn," I said shakin' my head. "That's one lucky bitch."

THURSDAY, 2:33 PM

****

Sometimes I think the world hates me. Cuz the bitch stay puttin' me in fucked up situations.

-Kelsi

I couldn't believe these dudes.

We was supposed to be puttin' in work for Kyope, and these mothafuckas wanted to stop by McDonalds to get somethin' to eat, prolly Happy Meals an shit. Bad 'nough Kyope ain't give me no details 'bout what we was sposed to be doin'.

I did know he was meetin' up wit' Jarvis and judgin' by the tone in his voice, shit wasn't goin' be sweet. I guess breakin' down that Brooklyn factory did exactly what it was sposed to do. Put a dent in they bond.

Wit' every muthafuckin' day, I was gainin' Kyope's trust. My work wasn't hard eitha, especially wit' Jarvis not carrin' his weight. Kyope was placing trust in me and losin' trust in Jarvis. Maybe he was tryin' to groom a muthafucka to take over for him so he could eventually get out the game. Only if he knew. I was far from the son figure he envisioned.

I was already settled in my new spot in Queens, and nobody knew where I laid my head, not even Kyope. As far as he knew, I was stayin' in a cheap ass motel 'til I got a place I could afford. He didn't press the issue. The only person who did was Kenosha. She was dead set on gettin' details 'bout where I laid. She been jive actin' desperate and it made me wonder 'bout her.

"You want somethin', Aven," Spikes yelled to me from the driver's seat. I was sittin' next to Crane in the backseat. I just stared out the window of the black Yukon Denali thinkin' 'bout my next move. "Yo, Aven," Spikes yelled again. "You want somethin' or not?"

He had wakened me outta my zone. "Oh...uh...naw. I'm straight," I responded.

"What 'bout you, Crane?" Spikes mouthed to him in the rearview mirror. .

Crane wrote on the pad he carried around wit' him and handed it to Spikes. Spikes read it aloud and gave it back to him. Every now and again I could feel Crane's stares. This dude gave me the creeps. If he had somethin' to say I wished he'd write that shit down and get it ova wit'. Cuz for real, I was thinkin' 'bout makin' him next on my list.

"That nigga Aven don't neva eat," Prangsta said in the passenger seat. "I guess he tryin' to keep his girly figure together."

They laughed.

Ever since I busted that nigga in the mouth back at the club that night, he never got over it. He would say shit to insight me but I ignored him. I saw the bigger picture, and eventually he wouldn't be in it.

"I don't eat that shit...that's all." I was short wit' 'em all the time. Keepin' my words to a minimum for many reasons.

Number one, they wanted to know *where I was*

from…how did I find out 'bout Kyope…how big my dick was and everythin' else that ain't have shit to do wit' they asses. I was tired of bein' drilled. I eventually told them I was from Atlanta and the rest of my business was mine. I felt comfortable since O was from there and gave me a few specifics in case I felt inclined to give them. As long as Kyope was cool wit' my presence, they could kiss my ass.

"You dumb funny," Prangsta laughed after placin' the orders. "Food is food, nigga. You betta stop believin' that shit them white people be tellin' you. We all gonna die of somethin' anyway."

"Yep. Some niggas gonna die from bullets," I told him.

The entire car got quiet as shit. And all three of them turned around to look at me.

"A lot of niggas gonna die from bullets," Prangsta said. Everybody looked away from me. "But I'ma die from eatin' what the fuck I wanna eat."

"Then eat, nigga," I told him.

When they got they food, Prangsta grabbed a fist full of fries and stuffed his face. All while parked in the drive thru.

"I notice you don't talk much, Aven," Spikes said out the blue. "You makin' me think somethin' else up wit' you." His New York accent was so thick I knew he neva got out the city.

What are these niggas? A tag team? If Spikes wasn't askin' me somethin' Prangsta was.

"As long as Kyope's cool wit' me, I'm good. Plus where I'm from real niggas do real things. I neva heard the sayin' real niggas *say* real things."

"So what you sayin'?" Prangsta asked lookin' at me through the his sun visor mirror before he sucked back whateva he was drinkin' in his cup. "We ain't real niggas?"

Before I could answer, Prangsta angrily yelled for the cashier. "Hey! Get ya ass back out here!" Prangsta demanded.

He waited for the cashier to come back. It was apparent

our conversation was no longer important.

"Yes," she said smackin' her tongue irritated by the way he called her. "What you want?"

"I need you to get me what the fuck I asked fo!" Prangsta demanded.

She smacked her teeth before sayin', "What's wrong wit' it?"

I was hopin' she would take the base out her voice cuz I could sense unnecessary drama 'bout to jump off. And the last thing I wanted was to get locked up in New York wit' these fools, and have my cover blown.

"For starters you, bucket-head-bitch. I asked for a strawberry shake and you bring me a vanilla one," he said handin' her the empty cup. There wasn't a drop of shake left inside. *What the fuck was this nigga talkin' 'bout?*

"What I'ma do wit' this? You drank the whole thing," she continued shakin' the cup and rollin' her eyes and neck. "I can't do nothin' wit' this!"

"Bitch, take ya ass back in there and give me what I paid for before I reach through this mothafucka and snatch your throat out!"

She smacked her lips again and said, "You ain't my fava?"

This bitch was trippin'!

And what does this nigga do? He get out of the car snatches the chrome 9 from his coat, grabs the back of her head and sticks the barrel in her face.

"Open ya mouth," he said slowly.

She complies.

He slides the gun in her mouth; pass her lips and then her teeth.

"Now…take ya dumb ass to the back and get my mothafuckin' shake. You hear me, bitch?"

She nodded yes and he removed the .9 from her mouth.

"Look at this nigga," Spikes laughed talkin' to no one in particular. He thought that shit was funny but I wanted to light this mothafucka up. We spose to be handlin' business and was 'bout to get arrested on some fluke shit. "What you doin', B?"

All I know is if I got locked up and somethin' prevents me from murderin' Kyope and Jarvis, I'm addin' a few more niggas to my list. Suddenly my plan ain't seem so smart. I should've smoked these niggas the moment I got off the bus from Maryland and be done wit it.

Just when things turned into shit, it turned into diarrhea when the people behind us started layin' on they horns.

"What the fuck are ya'll doin'?" yelled the man behind us.

Crane must have felt the vibration of the car horns cuz his deaf ass turned around, and looked out the window.

To me, it felt like niggas in New York was real serious 'bout they McDonalds. I mean, didn't the people behind us see the bitch in the drive thru cryin'? And beggin' this fool to stop and take the gun out of her face? What was the rush for? This the kinda shit that be in the news and have reporters callin' it anotha senseless crime.

Still in the driveway, Crane opened his door, got out and walked up to the car behind us. Then he smashed the back window and stuck his gun at the girls head in the back seat while starin' the driver down. He couldn't speak but his actions spoke volumes.

"You got it, man!" the driver said. "Everything cool. We ain't in a rush."

"Please don't shoot," she cried as the chrome touched her temple.

They both calmed down and kept they hands raised in the air.

When enough fear was provoked, Crane resumed his position in the back seat wit' me. These New York cats be wildin'. I gotta shorten up they circle quick cuz I can see they dangerous together.

"My, nigga!" Spikes said givin' Crane dap.

When we finally pulled off, Prangsta and Spikes went on and on 'bout how they terrorized innocent people. I knew they were all high so I tried to let shit slide. But this was borderline ridiculous.

"Oh my, gawd!!! Crane straight punked that nigga *wit* his bitch in the car," Prangsta laughed passin' a blunt he sparked to Spikes.

He accepted the handoff and said, "Right! You shoulda blew his tires out!" he continued lookin' at Crane through the rearview mirror. He took a pull off the weed.

Crane smiled havin' read his lips and accepted the blunt when it was given to him.

The car was filled wit' smoke. Normally I ain't smoke wit' them but after the bullshit in the drive thru , when that shit came my way, I pulled so hard on it, I thought my lungs would collapse.

The moment I released the smoke into the air, I noticed our surrounding's looked familiar. Too familiar. Now I know I ain't been in New York that long, but I knew I'd been here before. When I looked around, I was certain.

I *was* here.

For two months at that.

When we pulled up into the hotel I stayed at in Brooklyn, a flood of fear overcame me. Did they know 'bout me and was bringin' me here to put me to rest? Am I 'bout to die wit'out seein' revenge for my Mom's death? I placed my hand on my piece and eyed all of 'em. Spikes and Prangsta seemed to be in a world of they own, and as always, Crane's eyes was glued on me.

He *did* know.

They *all* knew.

Crane placed his hand on my forearm and mouthed, "You

ready?"

Although the words couldn't exit his mouth, suddenly I knew I was overreactin'. The type of niggas they was, they'da murdered me a long time ago. Wit' no time wasted.

In the front seat Prangsta and Spikes was busy loadin' they guns and Crane began to load his too.

"You ready lil, nigga?" Prangsta asked me.

"Uh…yeah."

"Well you don't sound like it. You wanted to be put on, now you up."

"I said I'm ready. It ain't like I ain't put in work before," I reminded them. "What we doin' here anyway?"

"It's personal," Spikes laughed lookin' at Prangsta.

"You might as well tell the, lil nigga," Prangsta chuckled. "He need to know what he gettin' into. Since *he* might have to put in the work."

These were the most laugh-n-est niggas I ever met in my life. Did everything have to be funny?

"I'll say this…Kyope don't like nothin' or nobody fuckin' wit' his business. And his main man got a problem sometimes seperatin' business from pleasure when it come to the ladies. Last time he pulled this mess, a lotta shit got outta hand," Spikes said.

"You talkin' 'bout when he was trippin' off that bitch Helena?" Prangsta questioned, as he used a cloth to wipe his prints off the gun. Helena was my mother's real name. "That bitch was just as crazy as he was. That's why they was together so long. They said she could suck the fuck out a dick though."

Goosebumps appeared on my body. I whipped out my gun and pointed it at the back of Prangsta's head. I ain't even think about it, but I was sure I'd have to pay for. Still, they'd disrespected my moms. My reason for being here.

The car was silent. Their stares were on me.

"This nigga's trippin'," Spikes said.

"Bout time this nigga loosened up," Prangsta laughed pushin' the barrel of my gun away from him. "Come on, lil nigga!"

"Fuck that," Spikes added. "If this nigga act like this every time he smoke, he ain't gettin' no mo."

I couldn't believe I got away wit' that shit.

I tucked my weapon back under my shirt and exited the car. I was losin' control. I had to calm down. I might not get a break next time. I figured my mother was smilin' down on me, and as always, came to my rescue. I let out a deep breath.

Wit' all the drama, I did find out that Jarvis was the reason for our trip. And whoever he was dealin' wit' was interferin' wit' business and possibly stayin' at this hotel. Whoever she was, she was 'bout to pay for bein' wit' the wrong mothafucka at the wrong time.

THURSDAY, 2:59 PM

****

I know now, I'm not gonna make it outta the situation alive.

-Kenosha

I couldn't wait to get outta this hotel.

It held memories. Bad ones. And, I was hardly ever here anyway.

Most importantly, I made up my mind that I was gonna kill Skully.

I know this was nothin' like my original plan, but it was one I was gonna keep. He was in my way and would stop at nothin' to hurt me if he had to. And I liked everything about Jarvis. He was handsome. Rich, and obsessed with me. Skully may have had money, but he was mean, ugly and could care less about my well being. It was obvious that his plans for the future did not include me. So it wasn't hard for me to make my decision.

He had to die.

I couldn't believe Skully actually allowed Jax to rape me the way that he did. I screamed and cried the entire ten minutes and it did nothing but excite Jax even more. I'm sure Skully heard my pleas. So the next time I saw Skully, it was settled. I was blowing his mothafuckin' head off!

Pushing the curtains aside, I looked out the window of the hotel once more to be sure Skully wasn't watching me. I didn't see any cars out of the ordinary so I proceeded with getting my clothes together to run off with Jarvis.

I was almost packed when I heard a knock at the door. I was startled. And had to tighten up my ass cheeks just to prevent from shitting on myself. Hoping it was my cab driver, I looked out the peephole and the door was suddenly kicked open.

Two men rushed me.

One was tall and the other was light skin. A third appeared and than a fourth. And it was the fourth person who caused my breath to momentarily escape my body. It was Kelsi. Seeing him emerge from the doorway hurt. Our eyes locked and I could tell he was just as shocked to see me as I was to see him.

I felt him.

And we spoke without words.

He felt betrayed and me confused.

While I was looking at Kelsi, the tall brown skin man with a uniform walked up to me and covered my mouth. He was applying so much pressure on my nose and lips that I started to feel faint. When I managed to bite his index finger, he smacked me so hard my tooth fell out and hit the floor. He rubbed his hand that was dripping with blood and was about to hit me again until the tall light skin man with the dreds grabbed his wrist.

"Easy," the one with the dreds told him, tapping him lightly on the back. "I got it from here."

The uniformed man didn't speak. Just nodded.

"You probably wondering what's up?" the dreaded man,

started. "Or maybe you use to this kinda thing happenin' to you. You know, wit' you bein' a gold digger and all."

I remained silent. "It doesn't even matter," he continued. "You got into the wrong niggas pockets. I knew from the moment I saw you, that you were trouble."

Kelsi's eyes remained on me. I guess by now he knew that Jarvis and I was fucking. But what I wanted to know was what was he doing with them?

"We got orders to make sure you disappear," he continued before the butt of his gun appeared from his jeans.

Was I about to die? Like this?

And all of a sudden it was as if Kelsi flipped. "Yo why we wastin' time on this bitch?" Kelsi grabbed the gun from him and flipped it over. "I'm sick of you niggas wastin' time when you should be handlin' business!"

He hit me in my face with the butt of the glock knocking me to the floor. Kelsi was like a lunatic. His screaming and yelling frightened me even more. But for some reason, I could feel he was trying to protect me. While he was in full rage mode, a maid walked through the broken door.

"Is everything okay?" she asked.

The men attempted to cover my body which was lying on the floor.

"Yeah…we good," the light-skin man said. "Uh…can we get some clean sheets?"

He was trying to get rid of her.

"What is wrong wit door?" the woman persisted, noticing the door was ruined.

"We'll pay for it," one of the men said. "If you could just bring us the sheets that'll be good."

The woman left and I was terrified.

"This nigga makin' all that noise and now she saw our faces," the light skin man said. "Yo, Aven, you gotta finish the job."

Who was Aven? I thought. Without warning, the man in the uniform walked up to me and hit me in the face. I went into complete darkness.

When I woke up, I was in the passenger seat of a black Honda and Kelsi was in the driver seat. It was dark outside and we were somewhere I wasn't familiar with. When I lifted my head, I was in so much pain I laid my head back against the head-rest.

"What you doin', Kenosha?" he asked, looking ahead at the dark road in front of him. "I mean…what were you doin'?"

"I…don't understand what you asking me," I told him holding my jaw.

"I said what the fuck you doin', Kenosha?" he asked looking at me. There was a blank expression on his face. He looked crazy.

"I…I…met Jarvis, and by the time I realized who he was, it was too late."

"Too late?" he repeated. When I looked down, I saw his hand was on the handle of a gun. "So you run 'round town with my mother's killer, and you ain't say shit to me 'bout it?"

"Kelsi, please," I said softly. "There's a lot you don't know about me. A whole lot. And I wannabe honest with you about everything. I know it's too late for me. But I want to be real with you…now." His complete silence gave me the permission I needed to continue. "I'm not who you think I am."

"I know," he smirked. "Your ghetto-ness comes and goes at will. But I peeped that a long time ago."

I made a mistake. I forgot to perform for him like I always did. It didn't matter anyway. I was going to be honest about everything. After all, I knew he saved my life back there and if I was truthful, maybe he'd do it again.

"I know. I lied about who I really am, Kelsi," I told him. "I know a lot about why you here. I know that you hurting, Kelsi. You been lied to. And I didn't know what that felt like until now.

Somebody I thought cared about me hurt me too."

"Kenosha, get to the fuckin' point!"

"Kelsi...I know who *really* killed your mother. And it's not who you think it is. It was somebody you trust." I told him. His expression changed. He looked demonic.

"What you sayin'?"

"I...-," the first bullet hit my shoulder and I felt it rip my flesh. I looked at the gun in Kelsi's lap and it was still there. So where was the bullets coming from? Before I could think of a response, the next bullet ripped through my arm. The heat and the pain was unbearable.

Kelsi's eyes widened as he backed outta the car. Then he started busting at the person who was shooting at me. Glass shattered everywhere. Kelsi, missed. It wasn't long before I heard Kelsi's footsteps taking off hurriedly away from the car.

I was alone.

I was still trying to figure out the-who and the-why until I was pulled out of the car. Laying flat on my back, I saw the person's face that had been following me around since I'd arrived in New York. He had been outside of the hotel. He had been there when Jarvis made his nephew collect on his debt at Marcy. He'd been there always. There was no use in asking what he wanted from me. The look in his eyes told me he wouldn't tell.

He smiled, aimed and shot me in my face.

My blood filled my throat and choked me.

I was breathless.

FRIDAY, 9:02 PM

****

I don't make my reasons known 'til I get ready.

-Kelsi

I was in his presence.

Breakin' bread wit' him and his crew.

And all I could think about was hurtin' and killin' him and that white bitch he played close. Look at 'em, laughing and actin' like everything's fine. When everything in my world is crumblin' 'round me. I felt like burnin' his ten million dollar Manhattan loft to the ground. And even though I was able to put a dent in his operation, it ain't feel like enough. Maybe cuz I realize no matter what, it won't bring my mother back.

"I'm tellin' you, Kyope," Prangsta yelled as they all drank from the drinks they made at his bar. "This lil nigga's on his way. You shoulda seen what he did to that bitch last night."

"Is that right?" Kyope said as he looked at me. The smoke colored shades I always wore concealed my eyes. His girlfriend had her arms wrapped 'round his waist while her head rested on his shoulder. Everybody was dressed in all black, includin' me. "Looks like you one of my best investments."

I smiled and turned away. Whenever he stared too long, I'd readjust. I ain't want him to see who I really was by focusing on my features. I knew the hair on my face confused things a little but the eyes don't change. Even if covered.

"We couldn't even do what we was gonna do to her ass," Spikes added. "This lil nigga is thorough."

As they went on and on 'bout me, like I wasn't even here, I thought about Kenosha. I knew they was gettin' ready to kill her, so I tried to cause a diversion. Thinkin' fast, I saw the maid walkin' toward the room and decided to make some noise hopin' she'd come in. I was tryin' to save Kenosha's life. But what for? It's obvious she was a snake who deserved to die.

Ever since we talked, her words stayed in my mind. What did she mean by sayin' she knew who really killed my moms? It don't even matter. At the end of the day, she got what she had comin'. Turns out she had an enemy who wanted nothin' more than to see her dead. And who the fuck was he anyway? And why had he spared my life. They found Kenosha's lifeless body on the side of the road earlier today. And here these niggas were cheerin' me on like I did somethin'. Only if they knew that she didn't die by my gun.

Wiping her death out of my mind, I regained focus. Because the bottom line was ...I had plans to kill Jarvis and Kyope this Friday. No matter what.

Leavin' them alone, I walked over to the window and looked out at New York. I wondered what my mother loved so much about the city. To me things moved too fast. Everything and everybody was in a rush. Still glancing at the skyline, my phone vibrated in my pocket. It was O.

"Where are you?" she asked in her usual soft tone.

Although she was doing exactly what I told her not to do

by questioning me, the sound of her voice made me smile.

"What I tell you 'bout that shit?"

"You so predictable," she laughed. "I can always count on you to say certain things."

"You can always count on me period."

I don't know where that came from, but I couldn't take it back now.

"Look...I don't want to bother you. Just wanted you to know I was cooking, and if you came in late, your plate will be in the microwave.

"Good lookin' out," I told her. "I'll be there when I can." I ended the call.

"What you over there doin'?" Kyope asked. His question seemed out of line.

"Nothin...Just enjoyin' the view."

"Let me holla at him alone," Kyope said to everyone. His girlfriend kissed his cheek and disappeared into the back. "Have Rosa whip ya'll up somethin' to eat." I heard their feet scurry into the kitchen and Kyope walk closer to me.

"She's beautiful ain't she?" he asked, as he stood by my side and watched the city wit' me. "I've been here all my life. And ain't no place else I wanna be."

I just nodded. He was too close and I could feel my stomach churn.

"What do you want, Aven?"

"What you mean?" I questioned keepin' my sights on the city.

"I mean what do you *really* want out of life?"

"I wouldn't mind havin' somebody back I miss a lot," I said candidly speaking of my mother.

"What's her name? I'll have her brought to you by morning," he was confident and for a second, I wished he could perform the miracle. Kyope had the gift of gab. I'd give him that.

"Naw...I'm fuckin' wit you. For real, I'm just tryin' to

make money and stack money."

"That's it?"

"Yeah…what else is there?"

"You right about that," he confirmed. "But if you keep puttin' in work like you've been, you'll have all the money you want and them some. And bitches will be in line to suck your dick." I just nodded. This nigga made me sick. Why would he say some gay ass shit like that? "You gotta a girl?"

I thought about O, and was about to say yes. Spending these weeks with O made me feel like she was official. And every time I'd feel myself liking her too much, I'd pull away. To top it off, we still hadn't fucked.

"Naw…I'm just doin' me right now."

"Ain't we all?" he chuckled. This nigga's dumb.

"Hey…whateva happened to that bitch at Waves?" his question shocked me. "You know…the one that got my squad for their weapons?"

"What you think?" I said wit'out lyin'.

He laughed. Wit' all the mothafuckas I merked in his name, I knew there was no reason for him to doubt that I killed O. He ain't have to know she was in my crib cleanin' and cookin' for me.

"Good lookin'," he said looking back out the window. "So how did things go at the motel?"

"You heard 'em, I merked that bitch."

"I know that," he said. "But how was it?"

"What you mean?" he was askin' broad questions and I wished he'd just come out wit' it.

"Sometimes I feel like I'm alone in this war," he told me. "And I like to know I got the right people around me at all times. So when I ask you how was it, I want to know if you think every-thing went as best as it could. You understand now?"

I finally got it. He ain't trust his squad a hundred percent.

"I hear you," I said lookin' at him briefly. "But I'm not

for snitchin' in shit."

"It ain't snitchin'," he said. "It's keepin' me in the loop."

"I'll tell you this...Prangsta ain't as hard as you think he is. To me he was actin' nervous. Like he was afraid to pull the trigger."

"What you mean, afraid?"

"I don't know if he was scared, but he was procrastinatin' and I ain't go out there for the procrastinatin' and shit. So I put shit down how I thought you wanted it done. And just like you wanted, she out the picture, permanently." I could tell he was still thinkin' 'bout the possibility of Prangsta bein' weak. I was smilin' inside cuz it was growin' too easy to break his crew down.

"I need more men like you," he said lookin' out the window again. "Can't neva have enough loyal niggas on your team. Let's drink," he said walkin' to the bar, returnin' wit' a warm glass of Remy Cru. "To New York City, money and loyalty." I accepted the glass and did all I could do to prevent from throwin' the liquid in his face.

"To New York!"? I replied, afterwards swallowin' everything before needin' some more.

The moment I allowed the warmth of the liquid to relax me, the front door to the loft flew open and a man who looked familiar rushed toward Kyope. His maid ran behind him lookin' frazzled.

"Sorry, boss! He pushed his way in!"

"Don't worry, Rosa," Kyope assured, puttin' his hand out. "I got it from here."

I hadn't seen him since I was a kid but I still knew it was Jarvis. Even when Skully gave me his pic, for some reason, he didn't look familiar. And when I watched him, it was always from a far. But now...here in his presence, I could honestly say that I remember him.

"Fuck is your problem, man?!" Kyope asked right before

Jarvis knocked him to the floor.

Jarvis was high and it showed. I knew I said I would wait until the right time to kill him but when I saw his face, I saw red. I was too close to conceal my anger. When I knocked him down, my shades flew off. It didn't stop my blows. One after the other. I was splittin' his face. It took me a second to realize he saw my eyes. The same eyes that at one point needed him to be a father even though we ain't share the same blood. But I could tell when he looked at me. I was a stranger to him. I realized then that he never gave a fuck 'bout me or my mother. How could he and not know my name?

Wrappin' my hands 'round his throat, I pretended to be protectin' Kyope. Pretended to be doin' my job as a member of his crew. Jarvis's tongue flew outta his mouth and I could feel his throat close in. He was grabbin' at my hands and scratchin' my flesh. His throat was soft and flexible and all I wanted to do was bend it.

His eyes rolled back in his head as he attempted to stop me. I smiled. A warm blanket of satisfaction took over. And as easily as I was takin' his life, I was lifted off of him…suddenly.

"Easy, man," Spikes said as he and Prangsta held me. "Everything's cool."

Jarvis stood up tryin' to find his balance while rubbin' his throat. He was bent over like he had to throw up. His lips were bloody and his eye was already showin' signs of bruisin'.

"Damn, Kyope!" Prangsta joked. "You got yourself a stone cold killa. This nigga worst than me." When I turned around to look at Kyope, he smiled. I could tell he liked how I almost took Jarvis's life.

"Who da fuck is this, nigga?" Jarvis asked pointin' at me wit' one hand on his knee.

"He's new," Kyope offered. "If you had taken your head out that bitch pussy, you would've met him a long time ago." Jarvis looked at me like he wanted to kill me.

"I'll deal wit this nigga later," he said.

"Whenever you're ready just make a move," I told him.

"Easy," Kyope smirked, talking to us both. "Everybody calm down."

We backed down and I knew we'd have our moment again sooner than later.

"Why the fuck would ya'll kill that girl?" Jarvis asked lookin delirious. He must've fallen victim to Kenosha's power. I played her games before. But her control over me was isolated to the bedroom. He must've allowed her to enter his mind. "That was fucked up, man! You coulda talked to me 'bout it first! Why you have to kill her?"

"Do you hear yourself?" Kyope said angrily. "Our operation is fallin' apart! We losin' millions of dollars! Niggas is takin' us for a joke and the only thing you can think about is that bitch?!" This was the first time I saw Kyope blow up. And I understood how easy it was to lose control.

Jarvis looked at Kyope and then the rest of us. It was like he finally caught on to the severity of situation. Wit' one hand on his hip and the other on his head, he walked to the window.

"Hey…let me holla at Jarvis for a minute," Kyope said to no one in particular. We walked toward the kitchen 'til he yelled, "Aven."

"Yeah?" I said turnin' around.

"Stay."

I looked at Prangsta, Spikes and Crane. They hunched their shoulders and left us alone.

"Why he still here?" Jarvis asked.

"Cuz I asked him to stay."

"Do you even know this nigga?" he talked as if I wasn't in the room.

"I know him betta than I know you lately." Jarvis shook his head in irritation. "So you gonna ask 'bout him, or tell me why you been out of it?"

"I got a lot on my mind, man," Jarvis said lookin' down before lookin' at me again. "A lot of shit been happenin'. I can't explain it. It's like somebody's fuckin' wit me on purpose."

"What you mean?"

"Niggas been slashin' my tires, I feel like I'm bein' followed, I drop shit off to the cleaners, go back and it's gone. I think somebody been puttin' shit in my drinks when I go to the club cuz I been seein' and hearin' shit. I'm fucked up, Ky! For real."

"I hear you, but what the fuck does that have to do wit' business?"

Wow. I was impressed. The boy Kyope was straight unsympathetic to his man's problems. What I really wanted to know was who outside of me, was fuckin' wit' him. I needed to shake his hand cuz I wasn't doin' all that shit.

"Did you hear me, man? Somebody is deliberately tryin' to fuck up my life. And every time I turn around, I see this nigga as black as the night lookin' at me. He be followin' me 'round in a black Ford Taurus everywhere!" His description fit the one of the man who killed Kenosha. And I wondered was their situation connected.

"Nigga, we have a business to run," Kyope repeated. "I don't want to hear that bullshit! If you felt someone was out to get you, you shoulda came to me! Gettin' ghost ain't helpin' shit!" Kyope's breaths were heavy. "Either you help me put this shit back together or you cut! I'm not fuckin' 'round wit' you no more, Jarvis. The shit ends here!"

Jarvis looked like a helpless bitch in a room full of pimps and then he said, "I'ma do betta. You just gotta give me some time."

"You had three fuckin' months. Our entire operation has been reduced in three months. No more time. You start today."

"I'll get it togetha."

"Are you fuckin' around?" Kyope asked inquisitively. He

must've been thinkin' the same thing I was. He ain't have the look of someone in they right mind.

"What? Huh? Naw, man!" Jarvis said wavin' him off. "I ain't on nothin' but a lil' smoke every now and again."

"Cool, cuz my man Aven here is gonna be workin' wit' you," Kyope told him pattin' my back.

Niggas in New York did an excessive amount of hittin' niggas on the back and I was gettin' irritated. But I had to admit, I did like the new arrangement. I could have easy access to him now.

"I don't need a babysitter."

"You sure? Cuz I coulda sworn you just told me niggas is huntin' you down. Sounds to me like you need somebody watchin' afta you. Don't worry, he's cool." Jarvis looked at me with hate in his eyes and I matched his stare.

"Whateva!" Jarvis responded. "I mean, you da boss right?"

"I am." Kyope paused. "Now I gotta package comin' tomorrow. We changed routes. And since our shops been hit, we pickin' it up directly from Maryland. Nobody will know when it comes to New York but us. I'ma have Prangsta and them get it and bring it back. Aven here is goin' wit' 'em too. All I need you to do is oversee shit."

"But he new." he asked turnin' up his nose.

"Yeah…but already he doin' a betta job then the niggas that been 'round me for years. He goin'. It's final." Kyope commanded.

Jarvis shook his head.

"You can leave now," Kyope added.

Jarvis was on his way out the door when Kyope said, "And J, if you ever pull some shit like you did when you came up in my crib, it won't be shit left to talk about. I'll just be sendin' my condolences to your mother and whoever your new bitch is."

Jarvis slid out the door and suddenly I had another idea. The package wasn't makin' it to its destination. But I needed help to pull it off and I knew just who to call.

FRIDAY, 11:33 PM

****

The hardest thing to admit is that you wrong. That's why I never am.

-Kelsi

I punched the concrete wall so many times I was sure my right hand was broken. I couldn't believe I came so close to killin' Jarvis and missed my chance. I know I had a plan. I know it wasn't the right time. But what if I don't get the perfect chance again? I parked my black Honda in front of my buildin' and walked up the stairway leadin' to my apartment. When I grabbed for the door, I screamed out in pain. My voice echoed through the hallway.

"Aven, is that you?" O asked through the other side of the door.

"Yeah...open up the door," I told her careful not to let my hand come in contact wit' any object.

Keysha Cole's song, *Love*, could be heard a little louder

when she opened the door. She looked beautiful wearin' a red long shirt wit' the words Victoria's Secret 'cross her chest. And for a second I was glad she was there.

"Oh my God, Aven," she said lookin' at my hand all bloody from hittin' at the walls. "What happened?" She reached for it and I snatched it away.

"What I tell you 'bout askin' me questions?"

"I'm sorry," she responded softly. Her expression went from concern to anger. "I'm just worried. You come in here all fucked up and I'm not supposed to care?"

"No. You's sposed to mind your fuckin' business." I could tell she was hurt but I ain't give a fuck. I had too much on my mind to be playin' house wit' her. She walked away and I took notice that she wasn't wearin' panties. The girl was beyond sexy.

When I walked into the livin' room, the smell of candles, and cooked food hit my nose. I felt like I was home. O did things my moms used to do. She took care of me. There was always a home cooked meal on the table and if she had to work late, there was one in the fridge. It's amazin' the shit you take for granted.

"What you cookin'?" I asked as I took the clip out of my gun and sat it on the table.

"You sure you wanna know? Considerin' I can't ask *you* questions." She responded as most women do when they gotta attitude.

"I don't know why you gettin' mad. I laid down the rules before we started livin' together. I gotta go through this shit wit' you every night?" I paused. "You said you understood and now you trippin'."

"So the fuck what, Aven. That ain't the point!"

"Then what is the point, O? Enlighten me since you know so fuckin' much!"

"The point is I've given up everything for you. Yet you still don't trust me."

"Hold up, you act like I stole you from a convent and took your virginity. You was a fuckin' stripper! Stop feelin' yourself!"

"Whatever, Aven! The only time you want to be bothered is if you want me up under you in the bed. And even then you don't touch me. You treat me like I'm a kid! I got feelings too."

"A nigga can't win for losin'. I'm takin' care of you. I ain't been pressin' you 'bout gettin' your own spot even though I *know* you ain't been lookin'. Yet you in my face 'bout some bullshit! This is why nigga's don't move wit' bitches!"

"You treat me like shit, Aven!"

"Look," I started takin' off my timbs. "If I was treatin' you like shit, you'd know. Matta fact you wouldn't even be here."

"Oh, am I sposed to be happy?" she asked as she slammed ice cubes into a bowl. "Should I be smilin' cuz the man I care about don't give a fuck about me?"

This female is pissin' me off. And she don't even know me. Cuz if she did, she wouldn't be runnin' her fuckin' mouth! I had to call Bricks and I was in no mood for a fight. I don't know why I didn't just throw her out.

After a few minutes, O came out the kitchen and slammed the bowl of ice on the table. Afterwards she disappeared into the room returnin' wit' one of her brand new tiny white t-shirts and some peroxide. She placed the items on the table and aggressively pushed my legs apart. On her knees, she wiggled her small frame between them. For a second I thought I was about to get my dick sucked.

"Gimme your hand, Aven, before I hurt you." She said as her strawberry scented lotion filled my nose. I love a women who takes care of her body.

I gave her my hand. If she could fix this shit I'd be grateful, 'cuz I wasn't feelin' goin' to the hospital. There was too much work to be done. She took the cap off of the peroxide and poured it onto a paper towel. She dabbled the towel on my open wounds. It stung a little but she was gentle.

"I don't even know why I'm askin' cuz I already know what the answer gonna be," she said as she ripped the t-shirt apart "But are you goin' to the hospital? This could be broken."

"Naw... I'm good," I told her as she wrapped my hand in the homemade t-shirt bandage.

"I really wish you would, Aven." Instead of answerin' right away, I moved my fingers.

"Naw...I'm good. I don't need no hospital." I know she cared but right now, I trust no one. If I go to the hospital they may ask too many questions.

As I looked around I couldn't help but notice that she made this small joint a home. It was cozy and every time I walked through the doors, I'd relax a little.

I reached in my pocket and grabbed my cell phone. Takin' one last look behind me, I made sure O wasn't comin' back before I dialed the number. The phone rang twice before he answered.

"What up, Kels?" Bricks asked.

"Ain't shit. I got anotha move for us."

"For real? You mean them New York niggas not on to you yet?"

I laughed. "Naw. I'm still livin' ain't I?"

"You right 'bout that."

"Look...this lick won't be as good as the last one, but it'll be nice. It's definitely worth the trip."

"You know I'm in," Bricks said. "We got all D.C. on our shit now behind that last job. What the fuck was in that dope?"

"I don't know. They call that shit the "Crown" and niggas go broke fuckin' wit it. It's a killa, dude."

"Well if we can get our hands on some more of that, I'm wit' it. I still got your piece of the pie waitin' when you come back too."

"You broke me off?"

"Fuck you think?" he laughed. "Hold on, Kels. Yvonna, sit your ass down and chill out! We gonna take care of that shit! Calm down! Damn!"

"Who the fuck is that?"

"This new bitch, I met on my way back from New York. She fine as shit but she crazy as a mothafucka! I think this bitch got two personalities."

I laughed and said, "I heard that... But look, I'ma give you the details later. I just wanted to make sure you was wit' it."

"That ain't even in the talk. You know I'm down and so is my squad. Hit me when you ready."

"One"

SATURDAY, 1:00 AM

****

I got a sixth sense. And every time I ignore it, I have a brush wit' death. I'm listenin' this time.

-Jarvis

Jarvis sat in his living room going over the details of the pick-up with Prangsta, Spikes and Crane. This was a smaller package then they were used to receiving, but they wanted to test the route to be sure things were okay since they'd been stuck up so many times. Usually they'd have designated people handling this duty. But most of the people they trusted had been murdered. Security had been beefed up on the blocks but to Jarvis, it wasn't enough. Every detail had to be discussed to make sure nothing would interfere with the pick up. When they were done, Jarvis wanted to go over other matters.

"Yo…who the fuck is that kid and where did he come from?" Jarvis asked Prangsta. Everybody looked at each other as the topic of Kelsi was brought up.

"He came up to Kyope at Waves one night sayin' he wanted to be put on," Prangsta started rolling a blunt preparing to get blazed.

"It was that easy?" he asked looking at them.

"Well...not really," Prangsta said.

"Nigga, spit it out! How the fuck a new nigga get so close to Kyope?"

"He had this stripper broad lift our guns up off us," Prangsta said. "And-,"

"Not us," Spikes clarified cutting him off. "Ya'll niggas let that bitch get ya guns up off *you*. I smelled her fish ass the moment she wiggled it near me."

Jarvis looked down at them at shook his head.

"Well what happened to the bitch?" Jarvis continued.

"Kyope ordered him to kill her. And we ain't seen her since so we guess it's done" Spikes said.

"Yeah...it ain't like shorty ain't bust his gun before. He legit." Prangsta added.

"How come I'm just findin' out 'bout this nigga?" he asked sitting back in his soft leather recliner.

"Cuz we couldn't find you half the time," Spikes added. "But youngin' seem to be aight."

"Well I don't trust him. I'm tellin' you somethin's up wit' that kid. Just make sure when ya'll pick up the work from Maryland that you keep an eye on him."

"You not comin' wit' us?" Prangsta asked.

"Naw...I got some other shit to take care of," Jarvis said ignoring Kyope's order for him to oversee the trip. "Just watch him."

"What don't you like 'bout him?" Prangsta persisted.

"I don't know...Somethin's not right though. Just watch him, like I said."

"Got it man," Prangsta said pulling on his weed.

"I'm serious!"

"I got you, B" he repeated. "He won't leave my sight."

SATURDAY, 11:00 AM

****

In life either you're proactive or reactive. Nothin' in between.

-Kelsi

The drive back from Maryland had me homesick. It was weird goin' to Maryland only to turn around and head back to New York. I was anxious. It was just a matter of time before the details of my plan went down. I sat in the back seat with Crane, while Spikes drove and Prangsta sat in the front passenger seat runnin' his mouth. That dude was the best at bein' the loudest nigga in any area at any given time.

So Crane's mind-fuckin' ass couldn't hear my nervous thoughts, I pretended to be sleep. Seconds later, I heard Crane snorin'. Openin' my eyes slightly, I almost gagged on my own air when I heard Prangsta and Spikes conversation. I opened my eyes to be sure I was seeing what I was hearing.

"I know you not still mad 'bout that shit," Prangsta whispered lookin' at Spikes. They looked back at us once to be sure we was still sleep. I quickly closed my eyes and my shades hid my stare. "She ain't mean nothin' to me. You know we gotta keep shit up. You act like you want everybody to know 'bout us."

"Either it is or it ain't wit' us. That's all I'm sayin'." Spikes added.

These niggas was smashin' each other off? I can't believe this shit!

"Let's talk 'bout this later," Prangsta said.

"I love you, Craig. I love you," Spikes persisted. "I'm tired of standin' by and watchin' you disrespect me to throw everybody else off. And just so you know, niggas know you puttin' on a show. You not foolin' no one."

"You not thinkin' straight!" Prangsta told him. "Look how loud you are."

"I don't care anymore," Spikes responded.

I heard enough. I stirred a little and made enough noise to stop they conversation. I ain't trynna hear that shit.

"Hey…can ya'll pull on the side of the road. I gotta piss."

My announcement caused Crane to wake up and adjust in his sleep. He looked at me and pointed to himself. I think it meant he had to go too.

"Ya'll can't wait 'till we get to a rest stop?" Spikes asked lookin' at me differently. I knew he was prolly wonderin' how much I heard of they little conversation. I felt like sayin', 'yeah I know ya'll packin' each other's shit holes'. Nasty mothafuckas!

"Naw I gotta go now. I been holdin' it for a minute," I told him. It couldn't wait. Everything was timed.

"Aight pull up over there," Prangsta said to his undercover lover.

Punk mothafuckas! I couldn't stand naire one of them niggas now!   The moment Spikes merged right, I heard a loud pop and I was sure the tire was flat.

"Please stop playin'. How the fuck the tire blow?"

Prangsta asked no one in particular. I stooped down as far as possible in the back seat of the car.

Barely makin' it to the side of the road, we finally parked. And when we did, three bullets rang from the back of the car window shatterin' the glass. I ducked further before feelin' Crane's weight upon me. Had he been hit too?

"What the fuck?!!" Spikes cried out. I heard the sounds of they weapons loadin' in the front seat. "Somebody tryin' to get us!"

"No shit!" Prangsta said.

The shots stopped momentarily and allowed us to recoup. But when we did, three men in a black Caprice appeared on our left. They faces was painted white and black like the niggas in the movie *Dead Presidents*.

Traffic seemed to move along normally while the robbery was in play. When Spikes attempted to shoot, he received a bullet in his throat. Prangsta's eyes grew extra large as he witnessed his lover take his last breath.

"Fuck that shiiiiiiiiiiiiiiiiiiiit!" he screamed leapin' from the car. The goons began to fire some more. Prangsta fired but hit no one. I got a lil worried. I didn't want him to shoot one of my accomplices. 'Specially my man Bricks if he was wit' them.

"Nigga, you betta get in this car for them niggas kill you!" I yelled from the inside.

"Don't move, nigga," one of them said to Prangsta. "Unless you wanna be wet." Prangtsa remained still. "Get the shit!" he continued openin' the driver's side door then poppin' the trunk. "And watch that nigga!"

What seemed like hours was actually seconds. I felt the car shake a little as they opened the trunk. I smiled lightly. It was workin'. Now for part two.

I pushed Crane off of me in the back seat. He looked at me. Something about his mannerisms caused me to believe that he didn't want me hurt. Was he protectin' me? And if so, why? I didn't have time to wonder. While leavin' the car, he held on to my wrist. He was preventin' me from leavin'.

"Let me go!" I yelled in his face. "Whoever that is ain't 'bout to get away!" I finally escaped his hold.

Prangsta saw what I was doin' and ran behind me. I carjacked a woman who sat startled in a navy blue Pontiac Grand Prix. She had stopped to watch the shoot-out and now would become a part of the show. That's what she get for rubberneckin'. Other cars whizzed up and down the road stealin' brief stares.

"Move over!" I told her pointin' to the passenger seat. She complied while cryin'.

"Please don't kill me. Please!"

I slid in and ignored her. When I saw Prangsta runnin' for the car, I pulled off speedily in the direction of the Caprice. Lookin' in the rearview mirror, I saw Prangsta raise his hands in the air before droppin' them by his sides. I jumped out a few miles up the road and met Bricks at our designated spot. Another hot plan completed.

SUNDAY, 12:00 AM

****

Believe no one and trust no one.

-Jarvis

Prangsta, Crane and Jarvis sat on Kyope's couch. The package was gone and already their soldiers were complaining. Customers were going elsewhere to cop.

"I'm tellin' you, Kyope, that lil nigga set this shit up!" Jarvis yelled, as he got up from the couch to pace the living room floor.

"I don't think so, man," Kyope said.

"Why do you trust this lil nigga so much? It ain't natural!" Jarvis persisted, growing frustrated.

"You don't know what you talkin' about," Kyope said.

"Oh I don't? Are you sure? I heard about where you met the dude. So excuse me for not respectin' your business practices."

"Easy, Jarvis," Kyope warned with raised eyebrows. "I ain't too sure this fuck up ain't your fault. Whoever this nigga is that been followin' you was 'round long before Aven came in the picture."

"This shit here was an inside job! And maybe Aven been 'round the entire time and we ain't know."

"Inside huh?" Kyope was implying that Jarvis could be a part of the heist.

"Yes! Inside! Now I know I've been out of it lately, but I'm back now. And I'm tellin' you, I smell a rat! We should slump that lil nigga and be done wit' it."

Kyope walked around the living room while Prangsta and Crane looked up at him from the couch. Prangsta who grieved alone over the lost of his lover Spikes, was silent. He didn't want any attention brought to him since he let the robbers get away.

"Fuck! This don't make sense," Kyope replied shaking his head. "Somethin' else goin' on here. And I thought I told you to be there."

"I couldn't, man. I had to take care of somethin' else."

"Somethin' else like what?! You makin' too many fuckin' excuses. And instead of dealin' wit' it business and ownin' up when you drop the ball, you blamin' otha mothafuckas!" Kyope yelled. Just when he spoke, Kyope's maid advised him that Aven was at the door. They all looked at each other in shock. If Aven was involved, they figured he'd be long gone by now. "Let him in!" Kyope said rushing toward her.

Seconds later Aven came walking in. Visibly beaten but okay.

"Fuck is up, kid?" Kyope said, still hoping his potential protégé' hadn't betrayed him.

"I went after the guys who stole the package," Aven told him.

"You went after the guys who got the package?" Jarvis laughed. "Fuck you talkin' 'bout?"

"Just what I said," Aven said slowly. "When them moth-afuckas took our shit I jacked a car and went after 'em. Prangsta saw me. Ask him."

"He did go after them," Prangsta responded. "But that's all I saw."

"I know you don't believe this lil nigga, Kyope. Come on, man...please say you can see through his bullshit," Jarvis chuckled. "He went after them but he ain't got no package." Kyope scratched his head and mentally agreed with Jarvis.

"If you went after them like you said you did," he said slowly. "Where is the package? And why you still breathin'?" Aven went into the hallway and grabbed a blue bag.

"I got back what I could, the rest is in my car," he paused and looked at Jarvis. And I'm still alive cuz I'm a soldier."

"Got back what you could, huh?" Jarvis laughed. "Kyope if you don't kill this mothafucka I will."

"You ain't doin' shit!"

Kyope lifted the bag off the floor and looked at Jarvis who walked toward the window. After examining the bag, he was relieved that he had some weight.

"The rest is in the car?"

"Yeah. You can go see."

"Go check, Prangsta."

Slicing one of the packages open with a knife, he dug into the plastic and broke it. Afterwards he went into the kitchen and grabbed a kit he used to test his product. Adding a little liquid, he smiled when it turned red. It was good.

"How you get it back?" Kyope asked as if it mattered.

"Can I talk to you about that alone? Please?" Aven asked.

"Sure," he said finally acknowledging everyone else in the room. "Everybody get the fuck out."

"I'm staying," Jarvis rebutted.

"Get the fuck outta here, Jarvis. Let me talk to him alone."

They all left but not before Jarvis mugged Kelsi. He had plans for him later.

When the room was cleared he said, "What's up?"

"When I caught up wit' one of them, I shot at his body 'til he told me who sent him. And he said, Jarvis. He said they'd been plannin' this shit for a week. Told him you not doin' him right and that he wanted to go on his own. They was sposed to split everything down the middle. But they wasn't expectin' me." Kyope was a little off balance as he listened to Aven's story.

"Finish."

"They sayin' that Jarvis been settin' up shop too cuz eventually he goin' fly solo. That's why he aint' been 'round. Man, I don't know how long ya'll been boys and shit, but somethin' ain't right. This mothafucka gave me names and everything. And I'm sure he was in here trynna tell you I had somethin' to do wit' it. I bet all of 'em was. And that's why I risked my life to get your package back. I'm loyal to you, but I can't say the same thing for your man. Think about his patterns. If you *really* feel this nigga's the same, then I'm wrong. But tortured men speak truth. And that man I shot up told me Jarvis was behind this shit. The nigga knew he was dead regardless, fuck he goin' lie to me for?"

Kyope walked away from Aven to think. Jarvis had been less than reliable at best. And he wasn't able to depend on him anymore. But they'd been friends and business associates longer than Kelsi was alive. But he wasn't the same. So it was settled. Kyope had to react. And by that it meant killin' his long time friend.

Aven looked at the state he put Kyope in and smiled inside. Sure he could've killed them both and be done but he wanted their minds fucked up. And when that was done, he'd put them both out of their misery.

Sunday, 2:45 pm
****

If you want some shit done you gotta do it your damn self!
-Skully

Skully had called Kenosha repeatedly. He figured she wasn't answering the phone after the beating he'd given her at the hotel. But as far as he was concerned, he'd given her enough time to get over it and get back to work. The longer he didn't hear from her, and the more he did business with Kyope only to find that Jarvis was still alive, the angrier he became. He hadn't even spoken with Kelsi.

"Sir, do you need anything else?" Jax asked, as they loaded up the car on their way to the NYC.

"Naw…I'm good. But I can't say the same for everybody else."

SUNDAY, 2:45 PM

****

If you want some shit done you gotta do it your damn self!

-Skully

I sat in the livin' room wit' Bricks and his brother Melvin discussin' our latest caper. I checked on O before we came into my apartment, and she said she was sleep. I just hoped she stayed that way. I walked to the apartment window to look out. I wanted to make sure nobody was out there watchin'. I ain't see nobody.

"So he went for it again?" Bricks asked sittin' on the couch wit' his brother. "This cat has to be the dumbest nigga who ever entered the game."

"I know, man. Everything went smooth. I'm just happy ya'll niggas got ya aim on point," I laughed for the first time since everything happened. It felt good to be amongst real niggas. "Cuz them bullets was whizzin' awfully close to my head, slim."

"I wasn't goin' shoot your, young ass," Melvin laughed. "I'm a beast wit' that hammer. Don't forget who the first mothafucka was who taught *you* how to hold."

I laughed. "You right. I'm just glad you ain't rusty."

"So when you gonna call it quits?"

"I'ma 'bout to end this shit in a few days. I'm tired of playin' wit' these cats."

"You never did tell me why you *really* here," Bricks said.

"I was thinkin' the same thing," Melvin added. "You out here on your own fuckin' wit' some heavyweights. You betta be careful son."

"Do it look like I ain't been careful?" I laughed. "If these niggas was so thorough, we wouldn'tve been able to get away wit' what we have. It's child's play."

"Yeah aight," Melvin said. His tone let me know that he felt I was overstayin' my welcome in New York. "I think you should count your chips and come back home while you still can."

"I am," I told him. "But now is not the time. Trust me."

"Aye, man…let me holla at you before we leave," Bricks said. "Melvin, meet me downstairs."

"Aight, moe, I'ma wait in the car." Melvin gave me some dap and bounced.

"Look…I wanna holla at you 'bout that Keisha thing," he said as he sipped his beer. "I don't know what she told you before she died, but I neva touched that girl. I would neva break our bond over no female. No disrespect to shawty since she dead and all, but that's my word."

I couldn't say shit cuz it was my mother who told me he was disloyal. She told me she saw Keisha and Bricks at a restaurant alone. And when I went to school the next day, I seen them laughin' it up in the hallway. I just assumed she was right. I wouldn't be surprised if moms got it fucked up though. Bricks was always a real nigga. Plus he openly made comments 'bout how fine Keisha was. A nigga on some cruddy shit ain't settin' himself up like dat.

"It's all good. We ova that shit now." I told him ignorin' the issue. "It's 'bout dat paper now, man. I'm tryin' go back and live like a King."

"But you believe me, right?" Bricks persisted.

This nigga was blowin' me.

I wanted him to let that shit go, but he kept pressin' it. Right before I told him to drop the issue, his eyes grew big as he looked at somethin' behind me. My heart raced. Had I been caught slippin'? On impulse I went for my heat in my jeans and when I turned around, the barrel of my gun was facing O's small face. She threw her arms up in the air.

"It's just me, Aven!"

I turned 'round and looked at Bricks who was noddin' his head in approval. "You ain't tell me you had company," he continued.

I took a deep breath.

"Nigga, do you realize what you almost did?" I asked him puttin' my glock back on my waist. "I was 'bout to smoke her ass thinkin' somebody got in here."

"My bad," he responded givin' me dap. "On that note, I'ma roll. Stay up. And let me know if you need anything else."

"You too." He said leavin' my crib.

"Who was that?" she asked.

"Shawty, what the fuck I tell you 'bout askin' questions?"

She was silent. "You right. Look, I been thinkin' about us and how I'm always in your shit."

"And?"

"And you right. I should just fall back and enjoy you while I can. And since you are right, I want to do something for you. Sit down on the couch."

Her eyes were seductive and her mannerisms sexual. I

decided to play along. Anything was better than hearin' her mouth and havin' her question me 'bout my whereabouts. I was anxious. And I ain't been anxious in a long time.

Part of the reason I ain't sleep wit' her was cuz I wanted to keep a clear head. And sex clouds judgment. There was a lot of things I had to do when I came to New York and I wanted to be smart. I could get pussy anywhere at anytime. But now, since things were going well, I decided to take a little reward. O disappeared into the bedroom and I watched her ass wiggle in my white t-shirt she was wearing.

When she came back she had on one of her stripper costumes. It was hot pink. O put the lights on dim and turned the stereo system on. The Isley Brother's, *Don't Say Goodbye,* blasted from the speakers. She was fluid in her motions as she danced a few feet away from me. Wit' her back faced me, she made her ass cheeks jump one at a time. Takin' one look at me over her shoulders, she slowly whined. She was a pro. I smiled. She winked.

Bendin' down in front of me, she moved like a snake as she got on her hands and knees wit' her ass in the air. I could see straight through her outfit and inside that pink pussy. Suddenly I wondered how it was possible for me to avoid her for so long. She was the sexiest woman I seen in a long time. For the first time, I *really* noticed her. On her hands and knees, she moved toward me like a cat, ass windin' behind her. Now standin' up, she straddled me lookin' into my eyes.

"Aven, make love to me," she begged. My dick was trynna bust through my jeans.

"Pleasseeeee," she continued.

"We can't do this," I said as her mouth covered mine, but I broke the kiss. "I ain't trynna hurt you shawty. There's a lot about me you don't know."

"I don't care, Aven. I don't care. Let me take care of you. You won't be disappointed," she said pressin' her warm tongue within' my mouth. "Let's get away from New York. Together."

"You know I can't do that," I said in between heavy breaths.

She was a seducer. And a good one at that. Wit'out permission, she freed my dick from my jeans. I wanted to feel her. She lifted up slightly and put me inside of her tight wet hole. *Fuck*! Why did she have to feel so good? I grabbed her ass and pushed into her while she rotated her hips like an album on a record player. She was the best. Better than Kenosha and Keisha put together. I knew I was gonna have to hit this again before everything was all said and done. My jeans were soaked with her juices and I felt her tremblin'. She was 'bout to cum. It was good thing cuz I was 'bout to cum too.

"Ahhhhhh...please don't stop," she said softly. "I'm cummin'...please." I gripped her tighter and pushed as deep as I could in her.

"I love you, Kelsi."

It took only a second before I realized she said my name. My *real* name. Still, I bust inside her. She fell into my chest, her breaths heavy.

"What you call me?" I asked trynna regain control.

She took a few more heavy breaths before lookin' into my eyes. "Kelsi...I called you Kelsi."

I tossed her of me, cut the lights on and looked at her. Her naked body sat on the hardwood floor. "How you know my name?" I asked standin' over top of her pullin' up my jeans

"I heard your friend say it the other night when he called. Plus your tattoo says it. I always wondered what it meant." Fuck! I forgot about my tattoo and I forgot to tell Bricks not to call me by my government name. What bugged me the most was that she knew more than I wanted her too.

"My name is, Aven. Don't ever call me, Kelsi again." Her head dropped.

"Kel...I mean, Aven," she said standin' up. "I care about

you. I really do. But you won't let me in. I just wanna take care of you. I don't know who hurt you in the past but I won't. I promise. I'm not like that. Why do you think I haven't gone to Atlanta yet?"

"I want you outta here when I get back!" I told her as I grabbed my jacket and my car keys. "And if you still here when I get back, it's goin' be trouble."

"Aven…please. What can I do to make you trust me? I know you said you didn't wanna know much about me. But I wanna tell you anyway. My real name is Constance Brail. My mother and father-,"

"Bitch, you heard what I said?" I interrupted her. "I want you outta here!"

"Kelsi, please!" she sobbed ignorin' my demands. "I'm sorry! Please don't do this to me. Please!"

"Be gone when I get back or I'ma break your neck! I'm serious, O! Don't fuck wit' me."

I heard her cryin' when my door closed but I couldn't be concerned wit' that. She violated and I wanted her gone.

MONDAY, 10:10 PM

****

They all may be blind but I can see.

-Jarvis

Jarvis sat in his May Bach waiting for Prangsta to pull up on a quiet Brooklyn residential street. It was a dark cool night. He had a mission that he wanted him to complete and he knew he was the best man for the job. Fifteen minutes later, Prangsta appeared driving a white Mercedes. He was dressed in all black and his dreads were cut. He cut them to represent mourning Spikes. The cars were parked so that the driver's side windows were side by side.

"What you need me to do?" Prangsta asked through the window of his car. Jarvis could tell he was high. Ever since Spikes was murdered, Prangsta used alcohol and drugs to get by. And since his love affair with Spikes was secret, he had to deal with his emotions on his own.

"I see you cut them dreads out, that's a good look." Jarvis confessed to him.

"Yeah...thanks." Prangsta replied emotionless.

"Look, I need you to go to this address and grab this little bitch," he said handing him a piece of paper.

"What bitch?" Prangsta asked accepting the paper with an address.

"The bitch ya'll thought Kelsi killed. You know, the one who snatched ya'll tools at the club. She's stayin' wit' him. The freak, Jewels told me where they livin'. All I had to do was take this bitch out to eat and she gave it all up."

"Kelsi?"

"Yeah...that's the little nigga's real name. You thought you knew him as Aven."

"Hold up," Prangsta said looking up. "Ain't that Helena's kid?"

"Yeah...this nigga been playin' us the entire time. I knew somethin' was up wit' that lil' mothafucka!"

"How you find out?"

"I was throwin' Kay's stuff out my crib, and ran 'cross this journal. First off this bitch's name was Kenosha but I'm not trippin' off of that shit. When I read the journal and saw the name said Helena I had to get high. She was goin' by the name Janet. And get this...the boy Skully helped her get away when we tried to take her out for tryin' to rob Kyope," Jarvis continued. "She was in Maryland the whole time, man!"

"Damn!"

"I know, nigga. When I saw the name Kelsi, I remembered bein' at Jarvis' place. I knew I seen that kid somewhere before when his glasses came off. I just couldn't put my finger on it. I don't know what he want from me, but if he came all the way out here, it must be personal."

"Maybe he knew what you did to his mother."

"Maybe."

"So where Helena at? I can't see her lettin' her kid roam around New York alone."

"I don't know and I don't give a fuck. That bitch can get it too if she want it. And since her son want it so bad, he ain't gotta look no further."

"So Aven is really Helena's kid?" he asked shaking his head in disbelief. "Hold up…you think he had anything to do with all the shit that's been happenin' to us lately? You know, wit' the shops gettin' hit?"

"Fuck yeah," Jarvis continued looking away. "He must have help though cause it seems like most of the shit happened before he showed up. I haven't put everything together yet. But I figure once we get Kelsi's young ass, we'll get all the answers we need. I got Crane out lookin' for him now."

Prangsta felt crazy for believing Aven was on the up and up. He had actually grown to like the little nigga.

"What you want me to do wit' the bitch once I get her?"

"Bring her to me. Alive. I have my own plans for her. Whateva you do, don't let Kelsi see you. If he's near her, wait 'til she alone. You know he ain't got no problem bustin' his gun but Crane can handle his ass."

"I got it," Prangsta said. "It's war!"

"Nigga it's been war! Where you been at?"

MONDAY, 10:44 PM

****

I hate falling in love. It's like having open heart surgery while you wide awake.

-O

O sat on the couch trying to get rid of the headache she had. She'd popped several Tylenol and nothing seemed to work. All she wanted was for Kelsi to come back so she could beg him not to make her leave. She really did love him and believed when they made love, that he loved her too. From the moment she laid eyes on him, she was drawn to him. Whether he knew it or not, she felt like they were meant to be.

When she heard a knock at the door, she hopped off the couch and opened it without looking first. Prangsta pushed himself inside and smiled when he saw the white outfit she was wearing. Even though he fucked dudes, he loved to rape women. That was a weakness he hadn't shared with his lover Spikes before he was killed.

O made a run for the room but he caught her in front of the kitchen knocking her to the floor. She managed to turn around and stuck her fingers in his eyes. She had no intentions of going with him willingly.

"Shiiiiiiit!" he screamed as she dug further into his eye sockets temporarily blinding him. "Bitch, I'ma beat your ass!"

Now free from his grasp, she ran for the kitchen. She was going for the drawer to grab a knife but he grabbed her by the ankles, pulling her to the floor again. Nothing stopped her from grabbing the cast iron frying pan from the bottom cabinet to hit him over top of his head. She was winning the battle.

Although he maintained the hold he had on her, she didn't make it easy. Some kind of way she was able to get her thighs around his neck. With the strength only a stripper possessed, she cut off his air supply with her thighs. He squirmed like a fish out of water. Prangsta scratched and clawed at her yellow legs but she was relentless. She would not stop because she felt like she was fighting for her life. Prangsta felt himself drifting out of consciousness. With nothing else to do, he bit down on her legs until the flesh was torn from her body.

She made a yelping sound and she hopped up and ran for the door. Now he wished he had just pulled his gun out and killed her. Because now it was too late, she was down the steps and outside the door when Prangsta gave chase. Barefoot and scared, she turned the corner leading out of the apartment and was met with a blow to her face. She was knocked out instantly. When Prangsta turned the corner he saw Skully.

"Blow his brains out," he instructed Jax. "And pick up this bitch."

Jax complied and Prangsta was killed instantly.

"Wake up," Jax said smacking O in the face. "Get up, slut!"

"Uh…what…what's goin' on?" she asked finally waking up.

"You up?" Jax giggled looking at O's sexy body.

"What's goin' on? Who are you?" she asked nervously backing away from him.

"Don't worry about that," he said. "You're going to help us out. For now that's all you need to know."

When O looked around she noticed she was inside of her car. Jax found out which vehicle belonged to her by pressing the alarm button on her car keys.

"Now...we're going to take a little trip. And you're going to cooperate. And afterwards, maybe I'll let you suck my dick. Have you ever sucked a white man's dick before, sweetie?" O didn't respond. Warm tears streamed down her face.

"I know you haven't. But once you go white, you'll never go back."

"Please don't kill me," she begged. "I'll do anything, just don't hurt me."

"I know you will," Jax responded. "Now...let's go."

Right before they pulled off, Kelsi's black Honda pulled up. He parked in a parking space across from O's car.

Jax having seen a picture of him, knew who he was. Kelsi showing up now was not in the plan. They had surveillance at both ends of the street and he was supposed to receive a call if he showed up. The plan was to kidnap O, and place a call to Kelsi telling him that Jarvis was on to him. And that if he wanted O alive, he was to show himself. Kelsi was supposed to get angry, and go after Jarvis, finally murdering him. They were even careful to make sure Prangsta's body was removed and disposed of properly from Kelsi's apartment. Skully wanted nothing more than to have Jarvis killed.

"Listen...if he asks, tell him I'm a friend," Jax said seeing Kelsi approaching the car. "Tell him you're leaving with me and you'll be back later. If you don't I'ma shoot you in your stomach," he said pushing the barrel of the gun in her waist. "And then I'm kill him. Do I make myself clear?"

"Yes. Just please don't hurt him," she cried.

"Wipe your fucking tears and do what I've asked you too!"

"Okay. Okay," she sobbed. "Please don't hurt him. I'll do what you ask."

Kelsi parked the car and walked over to O's car. His face was sad. He never thought she would actually leave.

"Hi…Aven," she said as he looked over at Jax who was looking at the road ahead of him.

"Hey," he said, softly. "So you rollin'?"

"Yeah. My friend is gonna help me find another place. I'll be out by tomorrow."

"Your friend don't talk?" he asked eying the stranger.

"What's up, man?" Jax said looking at him briefly, before looking away again.

Kelsi felt something was wrong. And he took notice to O's nose being red.

"You sure everything cool?" Kelsi asked looking at Jax sideways.

"Yes. I'm just leaving, like you asked me to."

Kelsi didn't believe her. But what was he to say? He himself had demanded that O not question him about his whereabouts. So how could he question her about hers? And since he was white, and he didn't recognize Jax as being part of Kyope's crew, he pushed his feelings about the matter aside. Still, it was obvious he didn't want her to leave.

"Aight…I'll see you when you get back."

"Okay," she said pulling off slowly. "I love you, Aven." She took one last look at Kelsi in her rearview mirror, and pulled off.

He stood in the street and watched her, until she was completely out of sight.

MONDAY, 10:58 PM

****

If a woman steals your heart, technically does she own it?

-Kelsi

I drove 'round for hours 'til I realized I ain't have no where to go. I called Bricks and Melvin but they was already on the town checkin' out the clubs and the NYC night life. I started to meet up wit' 'em, but I had O's scent on my body and would have to freshen up before I left. Either way, I had to face her. And to be honest, I missed her.

But when I pulled up and saw her 'bout to roll, somethin' in me went numb. There was somethin' weird 'bout her friend too. But what was I gonna do? I spent so much time tellin' her to stay out my business that I couldn't get into hers. The bottom line was, I had fallen for her. I don't know how, but I did.

Walkin' up the steps to my apartment, the moment I turned the corner in the hallway, I felt some shit was off. And when I opened my door, my fears was confirmed. The pillows from the couch was on the floor and the cast iron pan sat in the hallway next to the kitchen.

My heart was beatin' damn near out my chest. I could feel sweat form on my forehead. They knew. They got her and they knew. And it was all my fault! I looked at her in the car earlier and knew something was up. And I still allowed him to leave wit' her. She needed me and I ain't protect her, although I promised I would.

I ran to my room to get my eagle ready to kill. I couldn't see anything happening to her. I should've put my glock to his head when I saw how he avoided eye contact wit' me. And when I saw the redness of her nose.

I was in the room when my phone rang. And I knew it was them.

"Kelsi...how you doing?" the caller laughed. It was the voice of the stranger in O's car. "Sorry for the mess. But you know how it is."

"When I get my hands on you, you bitch ass nigga, you gonna wish you neva said my name out your mouth."

"We'll see about that, but let me see what your girl has to say."

There was a brief pause before, "Kelsi, don't worry about me! They gonna kill me any-,"

Her voice trailed away and was followed by a loud scream. She wept in the background when he got back on the phone.

"I'm sure you heard what she had to say but let me tell you what she meant to say. I work for Jarvis and we're on to you. If you want her alive, you'll find me. You have a hour. Any minute after that, we'll beat this beauty of yours to death."

"You gonna wish you didn't fuck wit' me."

"And you gonna wish you never crossed that Delaware bridge. If you want her, find me. We're not hiding."

He hung up the phone.

It was time for war. The stage had been set and unfortunately, I'd have to play on their turf. This wasn't how I saw the endin', but I was up for it. That's what I came here for.

MONDAY, 11:22 PM

****

I always knew I'd die young. I just didn't think I'd die today.

-Kelsi

Bricks and Melvin made it to my crib in fifteen minutes. I briefed them on everything they needed to know and what they needed to do.

"Listen...I ain't goin' make it out. I already know. I just need you to make sure that if for some reason I don't kill Jarvis, that you do it for me."

"That's not goin' happen," Bricks said.

"I'm serious."

Bricks looked at Melvin and said, "How come we can't just run up in that mothafucka blazin'? That's what you got us out here for. I ain't drive this far for us to hand you over to them."

"I know...and I appreciate it, but that's how it's goin'

down. And I just want you to promise me you'll smoke this nigga if you see him exit this building before me. I ain't wanna tell you, but he had somethin' to do wit' my mother's murder. That's why I'm out here."

"Damn, moe!" Melvin said rubbin' the top of his head. "Fuck, you ain't tell us that first? We would've handled things a whole different way."

"That's why I didn't wanna tell you. I wanted things done slowly. Right now...them niggas is sweatin'. They let a kid come up top and rip shit up. Trust me, they not feelin' it. So I'ma go up there alone, and finish what I started."

"But why you turnin' over to 'em?" Bricks questioned. "Is it really over a female?"

"Not just a female. I'm feelin' shawty. You know I wouldn't put myself out there if I wasn't."

"I can't do it, man. I can't do it," Bricks said walkin' away from me. "I'm not 'bout to let you handle this shit by yourself, homie. It's not gonna happen."

"Listen, Kelsi. Let's think about another plan," Melvin started.

"It's too late," I told him. "We don't have enough time. Now I need ya'll to promise me that nigga won't make it out alive. Promise me."

Bricks looked at Melvin and they looked at me.

"If ya'll not gonna do it, fuck it, you can just hit the pike back home!"

"On my life...that nigga won't make it to the curb alive," Bricks said.

"Neitha will that nigga Kyope. I'ma smoke that fool myself. And that fine ass white bitch he got, too," Melvin said. "Just for GP."

"That's what I wanted to hear."

We was gettin' ready to leave when we heard a knock at the front door. I looked at them and they all cocked back their weapons.

"You expectin' somebody?" Bricks asked.

"Death." I told them. "But I doubt he knockin'."

"Kelsi it's me...open this door," A voice said.

I knew that voice. It was familiar. But what I didn't know was what he was doin' here. I told him where I lived awhile back cause I knew he was worried. He'd become somthin' like a father to me. I placed my heat in the back of my pants and unlocked the door. It was Skully.

"What's up, Kelsi," he said steppin' inside wit'out me askin'. "What's up, fellas." They nodded. "How's everything going, Kelsi?"

"Not too good, man. And I can't talk to you right now. Jarvis got my peoples and I'm 'bout to deal wit' him."

"Your peoples? Do you need me to do anything?" he asked. I could've sworn I saw a slight smile of pleasure come 'cross his face.

"No...I just gotta go," I told him as I bolted past him leavin' him in my apartment alone.

I appreciated everything Skully had done for me. If it wasn't for him, I would've never found out who murdered my mother. And he was the one who gave me extra cheddar to live out here even though I already had some cake saved up. But sometimes he acted like I owed him. Always wantin' to know where I was goin' and who I was goin' wit'.

I'm a sole survivor.

MONDAY, 11:58 PM

****

Murder is in the air. I can smell it.

-Kyope

Kyope had been calling Jarvis and Prangsta back to back. He'd even text messaged Crane a few times with no answer.

"Jarvis won't answer his phone," Gerry, one of Kyope's runners said.

"Try his house phone."

Kyope waited patiently in his living room although he already knew he wouldn't answer that number either. He was growing heated. He felt over the past few months, things were going out of control. And after meeting with Aven, he had plans to kill Jarvis. But how could he do it when he couldn't find him?

"Nope…he not answerin' that either. Want me to call the chick who keeps his nephew?"

"No…hang up."

He decided to pay a visit to Jarvis's place since he wouldn't answer the phone. And this time when he saw him, he had no intentions on playing nice.

TUESDAY, 12:22 AM

****

I finally understood what Biggie meant when he said he's ready to die.

-Kelsi

We parked blocks from Jarvis's crib so he wouldn't see me pull up. And I didn't want Bricks and Melvin, gettin' spotted. As I sat in the car wit' Bricks and Melvin a few blocks from Jarvis's crib, I thought about what was gettin' ready to happen. There was no need in procrastinatin'. I had to do what I came to New York to do. I was gettin' ready to get out when Bricks grabbed my arm.

"Uh…I just wanted to say…that it was an honor knowin' you, nigga. You one of the real ones." Bricks said.

"You too," I told him.

I looked at Melvin who was in the passenger seat. I guess I was givin' him a chance to say anything if he wanted to.

"I ain't got nothin' to say. I still believe you goin' come

back. So I'ma say what I gotta say when this war over." We laughed

"Aight...let me do what I came to do." Then I pulled my hoody over my head and left the car.

Walkin' up the block a few people looked at me and I felt like everyone had they eyes on me. I almost made it to Jarvis's buildin' when I heard, "Kelsi." I turned around and saw the same man who killed Kenosha. I placed my hand on my heat.

"Kelsi," he said softly. "I need you to come wit' me."

"I ain't goin' nowhere wit' you! Who the fuck are you?"

"You'll get all the answers you need, man. But I need you to come wit' me now."

"Like I said," I continued, backin' away. I would've bust his head open right there but then I wouldn't get the chance to help O. "I ain't goin' nowhere wit' you! So whateva you gonna do, you can do it right here." He walked toward me and I walked back. "Don't come near me," I told him. "I'm warnin' you."

"I'm sorry, man. I'm not goin' to be able to do that. I'm not goin' to hurt you. If I wanted to, you'd be dead by now."

I knew this fool wasn't goin' to let me walk away. Whateva he wanted with me was serious. So I was 'bout to take out my fire and smoke him, when I was struck on the head from the back.

When I came to I was sittin' in a hotel room. I jumped up and reached for my gun and it wasn't there. Where the fuck was I? I was just 'bout to leave when he appeared through the door again.

"You aight?" he asked.

"Naw...I need you to tell me what the fuck is goin' on."

"Sit down, we'll talk 'bout everything."

"I'm not doin' shit 'til you tell me what's goin' on," I was prepared to wreck this fool if I had to. Gun or not.

"Nephew," he said calmly. "I'll explain everything. Just please...have a seat."

TUESDAY, 12:47 AM

****

I guess all good things must come to an end.

-Jarvis

Jarvis made several calls to Prangsta but he didn't get an answer. He had a feeling something terrible happened to him, but hoped that wasn't the case. His phone had been ringing off of the hook and once again he saw Kyope's number. As he had the other times, he ignored his call and placed the phone back in his pocket. He wanted to have proof that Kelsi was a snake before he talked to him again. He was in his apartment having a drink when there was a knock at the door.

"Who is it?" he asked, walking to the door with his drink in hand.

"It's me," Kyope said. "Open up, man."

Jarvis took a deep breath, downed the liquid in his glass and placed it on the table by the door. Taking a look at himself in the mirror, he opened the door. It was time to deal with their issues. Once the door was open, Jarvis walked away without greeting Kyope. He shut and locked the door behind himself.

"So…what's goin' on, Jarvis? How come you ain't been answerin' my calls?"

"I didn't hear it ring."

"Oh really?" Jarvis said as he dialed his number. The phone rang in Jarvis's pocket. "Seems okay to me."

"A lot has been goin' on. I just needed to clear my head."

"So say that first. Fuck you lie for?" Kyope said, placing his phone back on the clip on his hip. Jarvis remained silent. "You've been doin' a lot of that lately. Lyin' that is."

"Like I said…I needed to clear my head."

"Clear your head huh?"

"Yeah. I was 'bout to call you though. Seems you not on your game like you use to be, Kyope. In fact, your game is some shit right now."

"Nigga, what is you sayin'?"

"Your man not as innocent as you think he is."

"Not this shit again," Kyope said. He knew he was referring to Aven. "When you gonna take responsibility for the shit you do? The breakdown in our operation ain't got shit to do wit', Aven."

"Kelsi," Jarvis corrected him. "Ain't got shit to do wit' *Kelsi*."

"Kelsi? Who the fuck is that?"

"Helena's, son," Jarvis said hesitantly. He knew that although Aven wasn't who he said he was, Kyope would look at this as still being his fault. Considering Helena was his girlfriend. While Jarvis thoughts kept him busy. Kyope was thinking about Kelsi. He remembered the first time he met him at Waves. He knew then that he looked familiar but Kelsi's warrior spirit blinded him.

"So why is he here? Fuck does he want?" Kyope asked.

"I don't know, man. I don't know what he wants. I just

know that he's here and he's been lyin' to you the entire time. I think he's after me for killing his mother."

Kyope paced the room and placed his hands on his head. While he was thinking about the predicament, there was another knock at the door. Jarvis looked at Kyope and shrugged his shoulders. He proceeded to the door looking out of the peephole. It was Crane.

"It's, Crane," Jarvis said. He opened the door and Crane walked in and closed the door behind him.

"Glad you here, man," Kyope said. "We got a lot of shit to handle and it's gonna be a long night."

Kyope and Jarvis were in mid-conversation until they saw the door swing open. Both Kyope and Jarvis looked liked they saw a ghost when they saw who walked in. Dressed in all black, wearing a long coat, stood Helena, or as the world had come to know her, Janet Stayley, Kelsi's mother.

TUESDAY, 12:47 AM

****

I guess all good things must come to an end.

-Jarvis

What he was sayin' had me fucked up. Speechless. We were in a hotel not too far from Jarvis's place. I could tell dude had been stayin' here because his personal items were everywhere.

"Why you fuckin' wit' me?" I asked him leanin' against the wall unable to support my own weight. My head was spinnin'. "If I was you, I wouldn't fuck wit' me."

"I ain't fuckin' wit' you, Kelsi. I'm your uncle and I'm here to tell you your mother is alive. I ain't got nothin' to gain by lyin' to you, young blood."

I looked at his ashy black skin and couldn't find a shred of resemblance wit' me or my mother. My mother was beautiful, and had almond colored skin. This man was unattractive and hard on the eyes to say the least. He looked like he spent a lot of time in jail and was goin' back soon.

"My mother ain't alive!" I said swingin' at the air. The possibility of it being true angered me cuz I ain't wanna feel let down if it was all a lie. "Stop fuckin' wit' me, nigga! She died months ago!!"

"No...they *think* she died months ago. But she alive, baby boy."

"B...but...if she alive, how come she ain't get at me? How come she let me go through this shit when she know how much I miss her? My moms would neva put me through the torture I been through!"

"Cuz she ain't want nobody findin' out she was still alive before everything was said and done. She wanted to make sure she protected her identity, but most of all, she wanted to protect you."

I rubbed my head over and over trynna understand every thing he was sayin' to me. My mother is alive? Can it be possible? I looked at him coldly. I wanted him to know if he was lyin', weapon or not, I'd kill him wit' my bare hands.

"If...if you really my uncle, then why you kill Kenosha?"

"Cuz she was goin' hurt you. Skully and Kenosha were the ones who shot your mother. And Skully made you think it was Jarvis so you could do *his* dirty work. You out here on Skully's bullshit, young blood. Kenosha was sposed to be makin' sure you went along wit' the plan. But she ended up findin' Jarvis by accident. I killed her to protect you. Cuz once you laid Jarvis down, she was goin' kill you herself."

As he spoke, I started rememberin' all the late night calls from Skully. And how Kenosha always appeared to have ulterior motives when she asked me 'bout my whereabouts. It was like she trynna make me angrier than I already was for Jarvis killin' my moms.

"Where is she?"

"Who?" he asked nervously.

"My mother?! Where is she? If she alive, let me see her. Let me talk to her."

"She's handlin' business, right now, Kelsi."

"What kind of business?"

"She 'bout to take care of Jarvis and Kyope."

"Alone?"

"No," he said calmly. "She got help."

I had so many emotions goin' on inside of me that eventually I started to feel naïve for believin' him. How I know he wasn't wit' Kyope and Jarvis and was fuckin' wit' me cuz of how I fucked wit' them?

"If my moms is really alive, tell me somethin' only she and I would know."

He smiled and said, "She told me you'd say that," he paused. "You killed someone in front of your apartment buildin', and she helped you cover the crime."

"Too easy," I told him. "Everybody already think I had somethin' to do wit' that shit."

"You and she killed Delonte and dumped his body in Ft. Dupont park," he added.

"Still not good enough," although I was startin' to believe him.

"The night your mother was murdered, ya'll had plans to kill your father for the insurance money."

That's what I wanted to hear.

"I need you to do me a favor," I told him.

"Anything," he said.

I hoped the nigga was straight up, but needed to know for sure.

"I need you to call my moms," I told him. "Right now. Please, man. I gotta speak to her."

"I'll see what I can do."

SEPTEMBER 30, FRIDAY, 10:40 PM

The hardest thing in life is knowin' your child's hurtin', and not bein' able to do a damn thing about it.

-Janet Staley

THE DAY OF HER SUPPOSED DEATH

Janet was shot by Skully as Kenosha stood watching.

"Let's get outta here," Skully said. "Before somebody calls five "O".

They were in an abandoned apartment building in Bladensburg, Maryland. Although no one lived in building for years, a few nearby buildings still had tenants.

"We just gonna leave her here?" Kenosha asked, looking down.

"Yeah," he said taking one last look at Janet who was on the floor with her arms tied behind her, and around a pole. "Let somebody else clean up our dirty work."

They left hand and hand, leaving Janet's soul to escape her body. When they left, an elderly woman who heard the gun shots walked into the basement. Like a few of the local crack heads, she came to tear the copper out of the abandoned building for money to support her habit.

"Oh, sweetheart," the woman said seeing her condition. Janet's face was badly beaten and blood was pouring from all parts of her body. When she checked her pulse, it was faint. She looked behind her a few times to be sure the shooters didn't come back. "Hang on, I'm gonna get you some help."

Reaching into her pants, she used a stolen disconnected cell phone that was only good for dialing 911. She had plans to sell it later for money. Janet was unconscious and sinking deeply into death.

"911…what's your emergency?"

"Yes…please hurry!" the fearful woman said. "A lady has been shot!"

"Where are you, mam? What's the address?"

"2151 Monroe Street, Bladensburg, Maryland. She's in the old abandoned buildin'. In the basement."

"Okay, mam. Can we have your name?"

Realizing she was probably getting in over her head, she ended the call and left Janet alone. She figured she'd done her good Samaritan deed for the day. The rest was up to them.

The ambulance arrived minutes later.

"This a damn shame," one of the male paramedics said. "I'm sick of comin' over here for bullshit."

"Nigga this your job," an aggressive female paramedic replied, as they lifted the gurney onto the ambulance. "Who called anyway?"

"I'm not sure but I think its crack head Hanna," he said pointing to the corner of the building. Thinking they were talking about her, she ran away. She'd been watching from the side of the building ever since she made the call. She wanted to be sure they came for her. "But who knows. It could've been anybody."

They whisked Janet off to Prince Georges Hospital Center's, Trauma Unit. They arrived within minutes. Because she was hanging on to life, she was unable to tell them who shot her.

And since it was an attempted murder, the hospital and the local police department was hesitant about releasing any information, for fear of her life. Months later, Janet still hadn't regained consciousness from the multiple bullet wounds in her chest. She was in a coma. Every other day a detective would stop by to see if she came around and their visits were all in vain.

Meanwhile, Skully had grown irritated with Jarvis and figured now was the time to play on Janet's young son's vulnerability. He figured by now her death had caused Kelsi all sorts of painful emotions. When he felt the time was right, which happened to be Christmas day, he killed a German Sheppard, removed its heart, and shipped it to Kelsi with a note that read, '*Nobody Has Heart When They're Dead*'.

On the same day, Janet came out of her coma. Realizing the police would get in her business, and ruin her plans to be with her son again, she pretended to have no knowledge about her situation or how she was shot. She claimed to have amnesia. And since not many people survived multiple gun shot wounds, it was easy to believe. Her plan was to get better, and find her son. She knew Kelsi would be in New York avenging her death because before she was shot, Skully told her how he would use Kelsi.

Every night, when the hospital rounds from the nurses were few and far between, Janet would get up and practice walking. Night after night she built up her strength without the hospital staff knowing. And when she was strong enough, she walked out of the hospital doors.

Her first stop may have been a shock to some, but to her it made perfect sense. She went to her old apartment building, waited until dark, and dug up a gun she'd placed there months earlier. Then she paid someone a much needed visit.

Nick Fearson walked out of the Prince Georges County, Homicide police department clueless that tonight everything would change for him. He was five feet from his personal car which was a few blocks from the station. She knew who he was the moment she saw his six foot tall frame, and his chocolate smooth complexion.

"Make sure you wear that little outfit I like," he said on his cell phone. He laughed, paused for awhile and continued. "Oh really? You remember the last time you said that." He deactivated his car alarm. "I had you bent over beggin' me not to stop."

"Nick Fearson," Janet said smoothly.

"Yes-," he responded.

It was the last thing he said before her bullet pierced his throat. She had to kill the detective. Because when she and Kelsi committed their first murder together by killing Delonte, Nick's friend, he vowed to make them pay. And she didn't want anybody kicking over old tombstones now that she'd regained consciousness. With him leaning over his Chrysler 300, she watched him slide to the ground. His murder felt good. In fact, it revived her. She was back up to her old antics. With no money in her pocket, she stopped by the only place she felt she could. Her brother's house. The day was one she wouldn't forget.

Janet arrived at her brother's house in Northwest D.C., early in the morning. She knocked three times before the door opened. The moment he saw her face, he was visibly shaken.

"Helena? Is that you?" her oldest brother asked. Having just gotten out of jail, he had that hard look. His skin was dark and ashy and he appeared unkempt.

"Yes," she sobbed.

The moment his recognitions were confirmed, he sobbed uncontrollably. He never got over what he did to his baby sister. He never got over how he raped her because their father made him for his own sexual gratification. He never got over how he watched his other three brothers rape her also to feed their father's sick needs. Abusing his sister was why he never was able to have a functional life. The two younger brothers were killed in a botched robbery they all participated in, and he and his middle brother were the only survivors.

"Yeah...it's me," Janet limped. "C...can I come in'?"

When she walked in, her other brother stood up. He greeted her as they watched her limp inside. They were happy to see her and were willing to do whatever they could, to right the wrongs in her life.

"What happened to you?" the oldest asked.

"It's a long story? Got time?" she smiled.

She told them about her run-ins with Skully and Jarvis. And they told her some things she didn't know. It was then that she learned that her father was murdered at a local cleaners, after the father of a young girl he raped, blew his head clean off his body with a sawed off shotgun. Hearing the news brought Janet to a gentle peace. He finally got the justice he deserved.

She told her brothers about Skully and Kenosha and how she had to save her only son. She knew she couldn't do it on her own. Her brothers, who were no strangers to breaking the law, jumped at the chance to help. Even if it meant sacrificing their own lives.

After all, they hoped getting their nephew back would give Janet some peace. The plan was well executed and they took their time with the details. To get the money to fund their project, the three of them robbed a few local dealers. When enough cash was generated, they decided to put their plan into action. Her brothers were none other than Cole and Rick Hope.

Rick was to keep an eye on Kelsi while he roamed the streets of New York, which he did. He would be in places Kelsi didn't even know. And because Janet explained how much she already hated Kenosha, coupled with the fact she tried to kill her, when he got a chance, he was told to kill her without hesitation. Rick carried out his duties perfectly.

Cole Hope on the other hand had a different job, which he also did very well.

PRESENT DAY

TUESDAY, 12:54 AM

****

The worse thing you can do is separate a mother from her only son.

-Janet

"J...Janet," Jarvis said stepping back. His blood looked like it was drained from his body. "How the fuck you get in here?" He cursed himself for not having his gun on him. It was in his bedroom, useless to him at the moment. Kyope stood in silence and Crane watched her the entire time.

"I let myself in," she laughed, looking around. Her hands remained in the black trench coat she wore. "Everything looks the same." She looked around and than back at him. He looked terrified. "Why the long face? You'd think you'd be happy to see me after all this time. Considerin' we use to fuck everyday for the three years I was wit' your worthless ass. That has to count for somethin'."

"Fuck you want, bitch?" Jarvis questioned.

Her phone vibrated in her pocket.

"Excuse me," she smiled holding one finger out. "This will only be a minute." She recognized the cell number as her brother's. She was still smiling until she heard the voice of her only son.   She stood quiet as he spoke to her. Instantly, her eyes watered and became red.

"I love you too," she said ending the call that lasted a few seconds. Only she, Kelsi and her brother Rick knew what Kelsi said to her.

"Where were we," she said wiping a tear from her eye.

"Helena, what you want?" Kyope asked, keeping his distance.

"I was in New York and decided to stop by," she smiled looking at Crane, Kyope and Jarvis. "I don't want no trouble. I was just in the neighborhood."

"Bitch, your middle name is trouble," Jarvis said.

Although she had a limp and small scar on her face, she was still beautiful. Not to mention her mysterious sexual appeal was on full blast.

"Helena, you got five seconds to tell me what's up?" Kyope added.

"Either way, you not gonna make it outta here alive," Jarvis said.

Janet laughed.

"Both of you niggas is funny as shit," she said looking at them. "You should know by now that I got nine lives. You tried to kill me. Skully saves me and then tries to kill me, but all of your attempts ended in vain. Get use to it, you lookin' at the baddest bitch who ever walked the face of the earth. And since my son played both of you like the two bitches your mother's raised, I'd say you met the baddest nigga, too."

Kyope had enough. He didn't understand how he even

ended up in this predicament, but he certainly wasn't going to wait around to find out. When her eyes moved to Jarvis, Kyope pulled out his Smith and Wesson and fired. The bullet landed in the wall. Angry he missed, he was preparing to fire again but Janet was way ahead of him. She whipped out her pearl handled chrome .45 and aimed for Kyope's throat. Crane immediately jumped behind her placing her in a choke hold. Her arm remained aimed in the direction of Kyope.

"Well looky, here," Kyope laughed. "Seems like you underestimated *us*. You should be smarter than that. Didn't you see Crane in the room?"

Jarvis was silent, and doing his best to stay out the way while thinking of his next move. And then he remembered a crucial detail.

"Hold up....," Jarvis said, slowly. "How the fuck you get in here? Kyope locked the door when he came in."

Realizing he may be on to them, Crane whipped his weapon out and aimed at Jarvis, Janet remained aimed at Kyope.

"Sorry, slim," Crane said, using his voice for the first time around them in months. "This my baby sis. Now lower that fuckin' piece, Kyope."

For a few weeks prior to Kelsi coming to New York, Crane legally known as Cole, worked around club Wave doing light jobs. When he wasn't doing janitorial duties, he'd act as a bouncer because of his large build. Kyope hired him the moment he saw him to protect him. The rest was history.

"YOU HAVE TO BE FUCKIN' KIDDIN' ME!" Kyope screamed. "I CAN'T BELIEVE THIS SHIT!" He went into immediate hysterics.

"Nigga, calm the fuck down!" Crane told him. "For I shoot!"

"I WANNA KNOW WHAT THE FUCK IS GOIN' ON?! NOBODY'S WHO THEY CLAIM TO BE!" Kyope's voice was high pitched and shaky. It was as if he was no longer sane.

He knew all was lost and didn't know how to deal with it. No longer caring, he was about to pull the trigger to shoot Janet, when Crane shot first. He hit Kyope in the chest. Before going down, Kyope managed to hit Crane in his arm, tearing the flesh from his bone. Janet now enraged, fired twice killing Kyope instantly.

Jarvis ducked to escape all the stray bullets.

"You okay?" Janet asked kneeling down next to her brother, still focusing on Jarvis. "Are you okay?"

"Yeah...just keep your eye on that nigga," he told her pointing at Jarvis who was cowering in a corner.

Worrying about her brother, but still remembering her purpose, she kept her target in her sights. She walked over to Jarvis who was crouched down near the floor and pointed her .45 near his temple. "Get the fuck up!!!You comin' wit' me," Janet told Jarvis.

"What? Bitch, you crazy!" he said standing to his feet.

"Right now you ain't got a lot of options," Janet insisted "Either I kill you here after we torture your bitch ass," she said as she cocked her gun back . "Or you can try your hand and come wit' me now, I'm countin' to three."

"Two-,"

"Okay...okay! I'm comin'!" he said angrily. "Were the fuck we goin'?"

"Shut the fuck up!!! I'm runnin' this shit. You'll see when we get there!!"

TUESDAY, 11:00 AM

****

She alive. My moms' alive.

-Kelsi

"I gotta get some air, right quick," I told Rick. The TV was on but I wasn't watching it. And I know he wasn't either. We'd driven in the night and were back in Maryland, not too far from where I use to stay with my mother. We were waitin' on my moms to call us, and give us the next move. "I'll be right back."

"I don't know if you should be out on your own," Rick told me. "I promised your mother I'd look out for you."

"I'm cool. Trust me," I said standin' up. "Since we not in New York no more I don't think there's nothin' to worry about. I'm good, trust me."

He breathed heavily. "Aight, but come back in a hour," he said. "Or I gotta come lookin' for you. It'll make me feel betta."

"Cool."

I was turnin' around to leave when I realized I had a question. "Hey," I said holdin' the door open.

"What's up?"

"How come you had Cole hit me?"

"Cause your mother said you was tough as nails and you wouldn't go willingly. I was doin' it for her."

"Oh...True." I laughed. "My moms always did know me."

"Be back soon, son."

I nodded and walked out of the cheap hotel off of Annapolis Road. It was funny. I was exactly across from Capital Plaza. It was the same mall parking lot where I got into it with Charles. I couldn't help but think if I would've just walked away, maybe none of this would've happened. It seemed like the minute we started beefin', shit went downhill. Fightin' over a female was the worst type of shit to get in. *Damn*...And I ain't even wit' the bitch no more. I had to kill her myself.

I decided to go 'round my old neighborhood. It felt good being back in Maryland. For some reason, I couldn't allow myself to feel too happy despite the good news. My moms was alive! The feelings I dealt wit', cuz I thought she was dead, were all for nothin'. When everything was said and done, we'd be able to go on wit' our lives.

I flagged a cab and asked him to take me 'round Quincy Manor. Although it wasn't my old stompin' grounds, I was hopin' my man, Jay was there and had some smoke. He kept the best weed in the Manor.

"How much?" I asked him.

"Eight dollars."

I gave him ten and told him to keep the change. I was in the Manor for only a minute and already saw some bullshit. I had to take a step back when I saw this guy stranglin' this female in a royal blue Suburban. Slim had her neck in a full grip, but she was stealin' the bamma over and over in the face. I had to help her. And then I thought about it. Who the fuck am I? I had my own problems to deal wit'.

Turnin' around I was bout' to hit it and leave 'til I stopped in my tracks. O came to mind. Had I gone wit' my instincts and helped O in that car, Jarvis and his friends woulda never gotten they hands on her. On the strength of O, I had to help this bitch.

Fuck!

Pullin' open the driver's door of the Suburban, I dragged the dude out the truck by his shirt collar. Then I punched him a rack a times in the head. I thought about Jarvis. I thought about Kyope and I thought about the white dude who held O against her will. I probably hit this nigga at least 15 times in the face. His lower body was in the truck and his upper body was on the ground. Then I looked at the shawty in the car. Although she was distraught, I couldn't help but notice how sexy she was. *And* she had cute toes.

"Hey you betta get outta here," I told her looking down at dude.

"W...why did you help me?" she asked rubbing her throat.

"I uuon't know. But unless you want me to change my mind, I suggest you get the fuck outta here before you be dealin' wit' your problems on your own again."

She must've got the picture because she made her exit and I noticed the rhinestone belt buckle she wore read, *Parade.* Fuck is a Parade? Who the fuck cares? When she ran off, I snatched the niggas eagle from his waist and shot him in the chest. Then I took his heat wit' me.

It's somethin' 'bout murder that moves me. I came to get weed and took a life instead. And I *still* felt high. Figurin' it was time to bounce, I walked to the main road to hit it back to the hotel. I was out less than thirty minutes and committed another murder.

Damn. I'ma fuckin' menace.

SKULLY

EARLIER, TUESDAY, 1:15 AM

****

Either she a ghost or the luckiest bitch I know!

-Skully

"You seein' what I'm seein'?" Jax asked as they watched Janet walk out of Jarvis's building with Jarvis in front of her. Crane was behind both of them before all three entered a car. "And it looks like Jarvis's man Crane is injured."

"She can't be alive! I pumped at least three bullets in that bitch's chest!" he said looking at her from the confines of his big body black Mercedes CLS 500. "She has to be dead!!!"

"It's been awhile since I arrested her, but I'd know that face anywhere." Jax said. He was a dirty cop with the NYPD who freelanced in crime in his free time. "That's her."

Skully was stuck. Never could he imagine she was alive. And although he didn't want to admit it, he feared for his life.

And Skully wasn't fearful of anybody.

"Let's drive back to Maryland. I need some more time to figure shit out."

"What 'bout the girl?" he asked referring to O who was in the back seat trembling.

"Let's keep her for now, I may need her for leverage. And if not, she'll be dumped at a truck stop on 95."

"I got detail tomorrow. I ain't been at the police station in days," Jax said. "I can't leave New York tonight."

"You *can* and you *will*. Unless you want your lieutenant finding out 'bout your extra curricular activities."

"Alright."

"I figured you'd see it my way."

TUESDAY, 8:58 PM

****

Seems that everybody I love is eventually taken away from me.

-Janet

The drive back to Maryland was long and drawn out. We had to make a few stops along the way because I was worried about Cole. By the time we came back, it was dark. I couldn't wait to see and hug my son. He was everything to me. *Everything.* I know some people might think I was wrong for puttin' my son in the predicament he was in. You know, wit' us killin' Delonte together. But I disagree. My only mistake was trustin' others. The next time we commit a crime together, our secrets will go to our grave.

"How you doin' over there?" I asked my brother who was in the passenger seat bleedin' to death. Jarvis was in the back seat tied up and lookin' stupid.

"I'm good," he said, lookin' at me. "How you doin'?"

"I'm fine," I smiled. "Just worried 'bout you."

"Hey...I'm your big brother. You know I'm good," he said as sweat poured down his face.

"I really think we should take you to the hospital." I was beyond worried about him. It ain't look like he would make it.

"You know we can't do that. They'll start askin' questions," he continued shiftin' in the seat. "Let's just get this over wit'."

"You somethin'," I told him rememberin' the good times we shared when we was younger. Cole use to be my protector. He use to fight anybody who tried to hurt me. It was my father who made him climb on top of me and rape me, repeatedly. I remember tears fallin' from his eyes every time he entered my body. He loved me. "Always tryin' to protect me."

"That's what big brothers do," he said in a low voice. "Protect they sisters." There was a moment of silence before he spoke again. "Helena...I'm sorry."

"Please don't. Not in front of him." I said referrin' to Jarvis.

"I have to. Just hear me out," he paused. "Awwwwww!!!!" he screamed in pain.

"Cole! You okay?!"

"Y...yes," he said, his voice tremblin'. "I'm fine. Just hear me out."

"Okay. Go 'head but try not to talk too much."

"I'm sorry for everything we put you through. You should know, that we always loved you. Always."

"I know. I know," I told him, stoppin' the sweat from runnin' down his face and into his eyes wit' my bare hands. "Just get some rest."

"You're a soldier. Look at the man you raised. I could tell in his eyes whenever I saw him, that he did everything for you. You...you...should be proud."

"I am."

"Tell my nephew I'm sorry I hurt him. Tell him I love him and that I'm sorry I couldn't be in his life. Tell him that it made me proud to see the man he became."

"Okay…I will," I cried. "Just please…get some sleep."

No longer able to dispute, he closed his eyes. Permanently.

The moment he did, I looked at Jarvis in the rearview mirror. This was all his fault. My stare was cold.

"I know you gonna kill me," he said defeated. I didn't respond.

TUESDAY, 9:18 PM

****

If I'm goin' die, I'm goin' out swingin'.

-Jarvis

When Janet finally stopped, they were on the football field at Bladensburg High School. Jarvis's curiosity was killing him. He wanted to know what was about to occur there.

"What's this about?" he asked once Janet stopped the car.

She ignored him and looked at her brother. A tear fell from her eye and she wiped it away.

"What the fuck is goin' on, Helena?" he continued. He could care less about her brother being dead. As always, the selfish man in him cared only for himself.

Taking one look at her brother, she knew his eyes were permanently closed. He finally re-entered her life, only for him to exit just as quickly. At least she spent enough time with Rick to get to know him all over again. She couldn't say the same for

Cole. The hate she felt enslaved her soul. Lifting her aluminum bat from the front seat, she reached back and busted Jarvis in the mouth with the tip.

"Awwwww!" he said tasting his cracked teeth. "Bitch, you betta hope I don't make it outta this shit alive."

"Don't worry, you won't."

Placing the bat back on the floor, she placed her jacket over Cole. Then she took a deep breath.

"I love you," she whispered. "And thank you for everything."

Getting out of the car, she pulled Jarvis out by his forearm, his hands still tied behind his back.

"Get the fuck out!" she snatched him, then slamming the door shut. She kept her gun drawn in case things wouldn't work out as planned. She reserved the right to shoot him if need be.

It took a few moments to walk to the football field. There were ten women along with Bricks huddled in an open circle, with flashlights on the ground for light. She smiled noticing Rick standing off to the right. As he promised, he got her only son from New York safely.

In the middle of the circle, stood Kelsi, wearing only a pair of jeans, no shirt. His muscles buckled as he cracked his knuckles. The scene looked like the one in the movie, "Four Brothers" one of Kelsi's favorite movies. Janet could not believe how much older and mature her only son looked in a matter of less than a year. The things he saw and did made him grow up. Janet made eye contact with Kelsi, winked and mouthed, *I love you.*

He winked back and did the same.

Kill him, she mouthed again.

I will, he responded back.

There was no time for fluffy emotions. There was still work to be done. Jarvis laughed hysterically noticing the scene.

"God is kind to me after all," he continued.

"Glad you think so," Janet said untying his hands.

"Don't try no stupid shit," Janet warned. "I won't hesitate to lay you flat."

"Try no stupid shit?" he repeated. "And risk whippin' your son's ass? Neva that!" he said shaking his head.

Jarvis rubbed his wrists and walked into the circle. Once inside, he stepped to Kelsi and looked him in his face. Kelsi removed his shades and didn't flinch. Like a prize winning' fight, they stood face to face. The flashlights on the ground illuminated the field.

"Let me get this straight," Jarvis said taking off his shirt. "I'ma get to break your ass off for all the bullshit you put me through?"

While he was still talkin', Kelsi hit him with a quick firm right knocking him to the ground. The grass rested in the palm of his hands. Jarvis balanced himself on one knee and hand. Then he brushed himself off.

"I see you mean business," he laughed in obvious pain. "I won't underest-,"

Again Kelsi knocked him to the ground. People within the circle laughed as Kelsi was able to get two hooks off of him in less than two minutes. This enraged Jarvis.

"Now are you gonna give me a challenge? Or just let me beat your ass?" Kelsi teased.

"Naw, nigga," he said getting up. "I'ma-," this time he caught Kelsi with a jab. Blow after blow they fought like animals. Kelsi thought about the stories his mother told him of when he shot her. He thought about how he hid in the closet when he was little scared and waiting for his mother to come back and get him. All because Jarvis was trying to kill her. He thought about the bullets in Janet's shoulder courtesy of Jarvis. Lastly, He thought about how he almost lost his life in New York.

Now…he was beyond angry. That's why he called his mother when she was at Jarvis's house in New York. He begged her not to kill him. He wanted the honor of beating his ass first.

"Get him, baby!" Janet yelled from the sidelines.

"Yeah, Kelsi," said Bricks. "Don't let this mothafucka get out on you."

Both of them were cut and blood poured from both of their mouths. It was a war. While the fight continued, Janet grew worried. Jarvis was fighting like a man who knew he was dying. Kelsi, was fighting like a man who was lost and now found. He didn't have the same drive. In a sense, Kelsi had less to lose.

When Jarvis got on top of Kelsi, and hit him with repeated blows, Janet hurriedly walked in the direction of the circle. Kelsi managed to put his hand up and look at her. He didn't want her to enter. This was *his* fight. This was *his* war. Believing she raised a man, she backed off.

Thinking about every man he hated. He finally flipped Jarvis on his back. Climbing on top of him with the little energy he had left he stole him over and over again. Jarvis was borderline unconscious.

"Th...this is for hurtin' my moms," he said stealing him again.

"This is for tryin' to take her life," he said again.

"And this is for O.," he added.

Jarvis didn't know why he was being punished for O because he'd done nothing to her. But Kelsi didn't know or care. Weak and in pain, Kelsi stood up, looked down at Jarvis and spit on him.

"S...so what now you punk, mothafucka! You not g...gonna finish?"

"Naw...I'm done. I got what I wanted from you. I ain't gonna kill you."

Jarvis laughed again.

"You just as weak as that bitch of a mother of yours," he said managing to pull himself up. Blood poured from every orifice on his face. "That's why I beat her ass the way I did. Ya'll can't fuck wit' me," he said deliriously pointing at people he didn't know. "I'm the king of New York! I am now and will always be!"

Kelsi walked out of the circle and to his mother.

"You can't let him go, K-man," she said, rubbing his wounded face.

He smiled hearing her voice. She was really alive.

"You right. I can't," he said. And at the exact moment, the circle closed and the women surrounded Jarvis. "And neither will they."

Kelsi turned around to look at the girls who earlier, helped him take down Kyope's major shop.

"Aight, nigga," one of Brick's girl cousins started. "I heard you like to beat bitches. And since you do, we got somethin' for you."

The girls closed in on him, and stomped him until the breath was removed from his body. Jarvis may have been the king of New York, but in Maryland, that ain't mean shit.

THE END

Come on now…ya'll ain't think we was gonna let Skully get away now did you?

WEDNESDAY, 7:52 PM

****

I ain't neva scared! Live by the sword and die by the sword is my motto.

-Skully

Skully was in his kitchen cooking homemade sauce for his baked lasagna. It was his specialty. Days had passed since he heard or seen from Janet and Kelsi. To say he wasn't tripping about the matter was an understatement. After all, Janet knew what power he possessed. She knew first hand how crazy he was, Skully thought. Even with finding out Kenosha was murdered, he felt stronger than ever. Now, he *was* a solo act. And although Kyope, his connect, was dead, he found another supplier. And he was sure Jarvis, his arch enemy, was dead too. But what did that have to do with him? He was his own man.

Placing a little more oregano in the sauce, he smiled

when he tasted the sauce. It was perfect.

"I don't know, slim," Kelsi said looking at Skully as he stirred the sauce with precision. "My moms would put a little more salt in there. But that's just my moms."

When he turned around and saw Kelsi standing in the doorway of his kitchen pointing a 357 magnum at his head, he was flushed.

"That's not true," Janet said appearing from behind Kelsi. "It might be aight." She walked fully in the kitchen and stirred the sauce with the tip of her .45, keeping a close eye on Jarvis. Then she licked the barrel sticking her tongue in the hole. "You right, baby." She confirmed. "It needs somethin' else. I think blood."

When she looked down to the floor, Skully was pissing on himself. Janet stepped away as not to get any on her.

"Not now, Skully," she laughed. "We haven't started with you yet."

"Janet, please!" Skully cried. He was on the same floor Janet was the day he shot her multiple times in the body. And just as he tied her arms around the pole in the basement of 2151 Monroe street, she did the same to him. "You know I neva wanted to hurt you."

"You funny," Janet said. "Real funny."

"Naw, ma! This nigga's hilarious!" Kelsi interjected.

"You right, baby. The man who shot me and left me for dead, is beggin' for mercy. He actually has the nerve to beg for his life. And he was tryin' to kill my only child. Damn, Skully, have some respect for yourself. Cause right now, it's not lookin' good."

"What they call this shit, ma?" he asked looking into the dirty ceiling. "You know…when a nigga gets what he deserves?"

Janet scratched her head with her index finger, using the same hand which held her gun.

"Poetic justice."

"Yeah! Poetic justice!" Kelsi repeated. "Yep, that's it."

"Baby, let's get outta here," Janet added. "I don't have time to fuck wit' him. I'm tryin' to live out the rest of my life happy. You ready?" she asked.

"Born ready, ma!"

Without further words, they fired eight bullets in his head. There was no way he was alive. Knowing their work was done, they walked out of the basement. Five minutes later, the lady who saved Janet's life entered and saw his mangled body which was tied on the pole in the same fashion Janet was.

"Damn, she really got you back," she giggled. The old woman remembered it all. "Karma, is somethin' else ain't it?" she examined his lifeless body. "Shit! Oh well...I'm told you got somethin' for me. Let's see."

Rummaging through his pocket's she found five hundred dollars in cash.

"Jackpot!" she laughed exposing her missing tooth.

When she left the building, she saw Janet sitting in the car. She'd been waiting for her to come out. The aggressive paramedic, who helped lift Janet's body into the ambulance after Skully shot her, told Janet when she was conscious who saved her life. And Janet never forgot.

"Thank you," Janet said as Kelsi sat in the driver seat. "Thank you so much."

"No problem, suga!" the old lady waved. "Just live your life!"

"I will."

And just like that, they were out of sight.

"What's on your mind, Kelsi?" Janet asked. Although everyone who'd caused problems in their life was out the way, he still seemed detached.

"Nothin'?" he lied driving on the Maryland streets.

"So after all this time, we lying to each other now?"

"No," he said looking at her and then the road. "I let somebody down and it's fuckin' wit' me. I been tryin' to put it out my mind. I just can't. I was really feelin' her, ma."

"Who was she? And where she at?"

"Her name was O, actually, Constance...Constance Brail. I know they killed her ma and it fucks me up cuz shawty really held me down. And I coulda done somethin' to save her."

"When was the last time you saw her?"

"She was wit' a white dude wit' red hair. He said he was wit' Jarvis but I ain't sure who he was wit' now."

"I know a lot has been happenin'. It's hard to tell who's who."

"You think," he laughed. "I'm just findin' out Crane was my uncle. That explains why he was always so overprotective of me."

"Yeah...he really cared about you, son. And he told me to tell you he loved you."

"How did you get over them rapin' you?"

"Turns out my father was the reason. They never wanted to."

"Damn...at least you got to be with them again."

"I know." Janet told him.

"Did you love her?" Janet asked, skipping the subject a little.

"I think I did."

Janet took a deep breath.

"I just wish I knew either which way that what happened. Feel me?" He continued.

Janet thought about it for a minute. She knew a man with red hair and he worked with Skully from time to time. And since Skully was involved, she was certain his muscle would be involved too. The only thing was...he lived in New York. She also remembered something else about him. He had a fetish for raping women. He tried to rape her once and she kicked him in the nuts so hard, she permantelly damaged his left testicle.

"Hit 95 North towards New York!" Janet told Kelsi. "I got an idea."

No questions asked, he complied.

Janet and Kelsi sat in the car and followed Jax on his way home from work. Her idea was far fetched, but to ease Kelsi's pain, to her it was worth a try. Jax lived in a quiet residential community in Queens. And the quiet blue home he owned, looked more harmless than it really was. Wearing his police uniform, he entered his home. And when he did, Janet and Kelsi bombarded their way inside with him.

You see, Janet knew what kind of man he was. She knew having a young girl at his beckon call, against her will, would be something he couldn't live without. She was so certain he couldn't resist, that she was *positive* O was at his house. And if she wasn't there, they'd have another causality to their list.

"What the fuck are you doin'?" Jax asked in full uniform.

Janet held him at gunpoint as Kelsi ran through the house. He knew his mother could handle her own. All of the rooms he entered were neat and void of any signs of O. And then...he came to a door which was not only locked, but also dead bolted. This was a room he wasn't allowed to enter. And this was the room he had to get in.

Running downstairs, he jumped in Jax's face.

"Open the door wit' the deadbolt," Kelsi demanded. He was anxious and had a feeling if O was alive, she'd be in there.

"Man, I'm not doin'-," was the last thing Jax said before Janet shot his hand.

"Awwwwwwwwwwwwwwwwwwwwwwwwwwww!" he whined.

"The next one's goin' in your chest, bitch!" she told him. "Now open the fuckin' door!"

"O...kay! I'll do it!" he said holding what was left of his

right hand. "Just don't shoot me no more!"

Kelsi grabbed him by his collar and pushed him toward the secret door upstairs. Reaching in his pocket, Jax removed the keys.

"You gotta do it," he whined. "You shot my hand."

"Aight...no problem, cuz. Is this the key?"

"Yeah...that's-"

"Thanks." Kelsi said shooting him in the head. He was done with him too.

"Damn, baby," Janet said looking at Jax's lifeless body. "You ain't no stranger to this shit are you."

"I learned from the best."

Kelsi was silent until he opened the door and saw O hanging from the ceiling by her neck with a leather black strap. A wooden block stood under her feet which she had to step on using her tiptoes to prevent from being hung to death. She was naked and badly beaten. Bruised from head to toe, Janet and Kelsi couldn't get over how bad the room smelled. Feces were on the floor and there was a red ball in her mouth which was connected to a black leather strap which connected in the back of her head.

The moment she saw him, her stomach trembled. She was crying and her sounds were muted due to the ball being inside her mouth. Not caring about the smell, he rushed toward her and helped her down. With the little strength she had, she wrapped her arms around his neck. She was alive. She was okay.

Kelsi removed the ball from her mouth and held her closely.

"I'm sorry, shawty," he said caressing her back. "I'm neva gonna leave your side again. *Ever*."

Janet smiled. Although she realized she wasn't the only woman in his life anymore, she was happy her son was happy. Placing some clothes on her frail body, they left New York and Maryland, never to look back again.

EPILOGUE

Kelsi, Janet, O (Constance) and Janet's brother Rick ran a small strip club in Atlanta called Heart. Rappers, ball players and the like frequented the spot for the classy atmosphere and beautiful girls. It was a change of pace from the cheaper and classless spots in the city.

"You okay, ma?" O asked kissing Janet on the cheek. Janet was wiping the bar down preparing for more customers. "You been workin' nonstop since the grand opening two months ago."

"I'm good," she smiled rubbing her hand over O's pregnant belly. "But I wish you'd relax. You a boss now."

"I know but it feels weird. I've always worked for somebody."

"And now you work for me," Kelsi said walking behind her planting a kiss on her cheek.

"You mean you work for me."

"Ya'll betta stop! That's how she got in this position now!" Janet giggled.

"At least you got a grandbaby on the way," Kelsi said hugging his mother next.

"You right. Somethin' good came out of ya'lls nonstop humpin."

They all laughed.

Although life appeared to be okay, Janet was still sad. She loved the comfort of a man and now she had none. Outside of Kelsi, she wasn't even close to a male. Truth be told, she trusted no one.

Until, about twelve midnight.

"Can I get a Merlot?" a handsome man wearing black slacks and a grey shirt asked O.

"Sure," she said politely. "Does it matter what brand?"

"No…but it matters who pours it."

"And how's that?" O asked.

"If it's all the same to you, I'd like that young lady right there to pour me a glass. And if she'll allow me, I'd like to buy her a glass too."

Hearing this Janet turned around and saw a familiar face. She'd seen him before but didn't pursue. Because the moment he walked in the club, women would flock to him. He looked like Billy Dee Williams in his prime. And he was beyond sexy.

"So what do you say? May I buy you a drink?"

Janet couldn't help but feel privileged. He never paid anyone any attention. He was always the one sought after. Pulling her shoulder length hair behind her ear, she smiled and looked at Kelsi. He nodded in approval. He wanted her happy and could sense her loneliness even though she never expressed it verbally.

"He's a good look for you," he said.

In that case, "Yes you may."

It was the beginning of a beautiful relationship.

Janet was enjoying the attention she was receiving from him until she saw a loud mouthed man enter the club. He was flashing money and speaking to the strippers rudely. Janet figured he'd be an easy target. And judging by his rude demeanor, it would be a pleasure taking him down.

"Excuse me," she said to her friend. "I have to talk to my son for a moment."

"No problem," he responded.

Then she got up and walked toward Kelsi. Without using words, since O was around, she used her eyes to look in the direction of the loud customer.

Kelsi smiled slyly and said, "What's one more body."

THE CARTEL COLLECTION

Wanna Become A Street Team Member?

Complete The Application Below

Name:

_____

Address:

_____

Prisoners Are Welcome 2 Join The Team, Too!

For Every Three Books You Sell, You'll Get One Book Free. Just Have The Customer Complete The Order Form and Write Your Name & Address In The Bottom Left-hand Corner.

Cartel Publications Order Form

www.thecartelpublications.com

Prisoners Receive Books For $10.00. All Orders Must Still Include Shipping Fees *Per* Book.

Titles	*Select The Novels You Want Below*	*Fee*
Shyt List	_____	$15.00
Pitbulls In A Skirt	_____	$15.00
Victoria's Secret	_____	$15.00
Poison	_____	$15.00
Hell Razor Honeys	_____	$15.00
A Hustler's Son 2	_____	$15.00
Black And Ugly As Ever	_____	$15.00

Please add $2.00 per book for shipping and handling.

Total: $_____

Mailing Address
The Cartel Publications * P.O. Box 486 * Owings Mills * MD * 21117

Name: _____

Address: _____

City/State: _____

Contact #: _____

Email: _____

Special Note:
Please allow 5-7 business days for delivery. The Cartel is not responsible for prison orders rejected. **We accept stamps**.

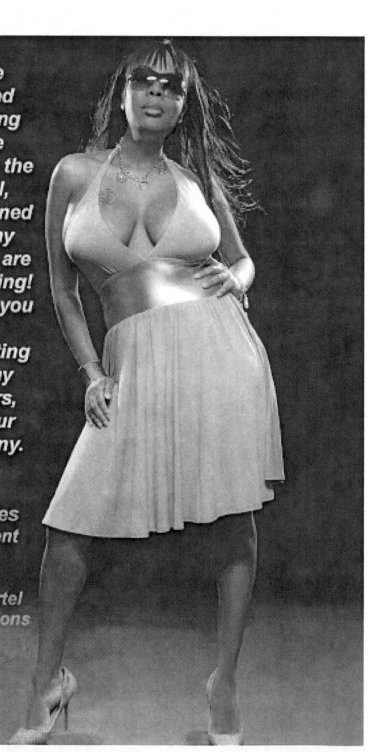

If I've learned anything since running the Cartel, I've learned that my readers are Everything! I thank you for supporting me, my authors, and our company.

-T.Styles
President
&
CEO
The Cartel
Publications